The Story That Teaches You How to Write It

William Gillespie
English 404
Professor Saunders
8 May 1996

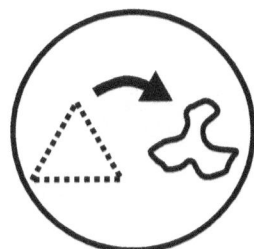 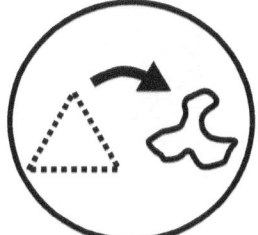 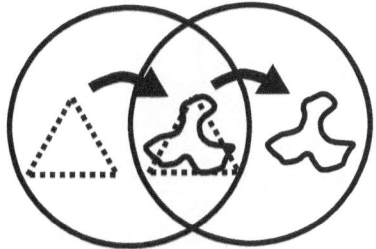

"The philosophers have only *interpreted* the world,
in various ways; the point, however, is to *change* it."
-Karl Marx

"The point, then, without doubt, is to change the world."
-Ross Chambers

LEXIAS	1	2	3	4	5	6	7	8	9	10	11	12	13
Semes	♪		♪	♪			♪	♫			♫		♫
Cultural codes			♪					♪		♪	♪		♫
Antithesis		♩			♩		♩	♩	♩	♩	♩	♩	♩
Enigma 1	𝅝												
"Deep in"		𝅗𝅥											
"Hidden"						𝅗𝅥							

Introduction: The Story Behind the Essay behind the Story

There is a half-smoked cigarette on my basement floor. Is that a narrative? There is a flat tire in the back of my car. Is that a narrative? There were no injuries and only minor damage in the blast at the building's main entrance, which police say occurred sometime between 3:30 and 5:45 a.m. local time. Is that a narrative? And another one of my feminist friends is getting married. That's a narrative, right? Augusto Monterroso wrote a short story entitled "The Dinosaur" which reads, in its entirety: "When I woke up, the dinosaur was still there." (42) Is that a narrative? Italo Calvino seems to think so (VIII). "Roses are red/Violets are blue/Sugar is sweet/And so are you." Is that a narrative? Shlomith Rimmon-Kenan doesn't think so (1). But I do.[1] "Water boils at one hundred degrees Celsius." Is that? Gerard Genette seems unsure (*Story and Discourse* 212). What is narrative? Answering this question, for me, has become the process of choosing the narratologist whose writing I like the most. After months of research, I have to admit that I don't know where or whether narrative ends.

But I know that narrative is the basic unit of experience. I know I use it to reason morally. I know that narratives are cultural, but I suspect that narrative is a cognitive process as basic as metaphor.[2] I suspect it is as important as (though not necessarily analogous to) language. But I don't know what it is.

On the other hand, written narratives—stories—I think I know pretty well. This is an essay about a story and a story about an essay. It all began with the diagram opposite.

When Roland Barthes rewrites the opening of Balzac's "Sarrasine" as a musical score, he raises a number of questions (29). For example, can this be performed? It is unlikely that anyone could read this score as "I was deep in one of those daydreams which overtake even the shallowest of men…" Is it possible, however, that another writer (having studied Barthes but not Balzac) could take this score and write the beginning of "Sarrasine" with different characters, a different plot, a different setting, but the same music? Can the various structural analyses of narratology be used to structure new, different narratives? What will this process reveal about the analyses themselves?

The separation between narratologists and fiction writers baffles me. Why would Barthes rather write a book-length study of another author's short story than write a novel? Conversely, why isn't *S/Z* used as a textbook in creative writing classes? Why would one transcribe music by ear if not to learn to perform it?[3] The aim of my project is to turn to the abundant resources of narratology back into stories, making the descriptive prescriptive, turning the model into a score. My attempts to translate narrative theory into instructions on how to write a story are part of a larger process of turning the world into instructions on how to write a story.

---

1   RS—This would be more compelling if yout old us *why* you believe it to be a narrative. Professions of faith don't carry one too far in a theoretical argument.

2   RS—"as basic as metaphor" is an interesting phrase because it suggests that cognitive "experience" is always mediated by a literary trope; which thus poses the question of whether there exists such a thing as "immediacy." WG—No. My wording means that metaphor *is* a cognitive experience, not a "literary trope."

3   RS—These are excellent questions, and, in fact, I wish you worked out some answers to them.

I begin the story with the following score:

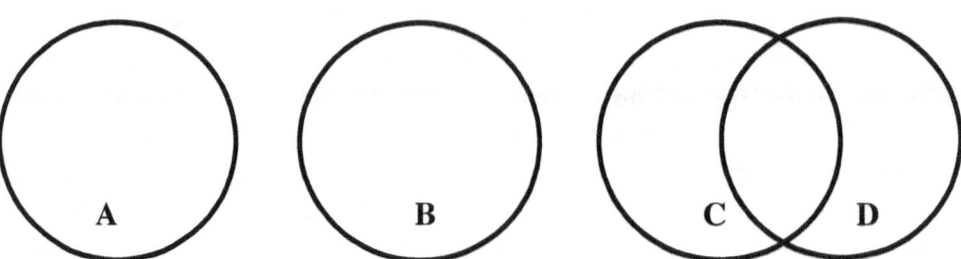

DIAGRAM 1.

This diagram represents four characters as four circles. The chronology of the story runs from left to right. The diagram shows that the story will concern, in order, four characters. The overlap between character C and D indicates that part of the story will be told from two simultaneous points of view.

Story / Essay Contents

A1. Genette: Iterative

A2. Lakoff: Character and Metaphor

A3. Genette: Proust

A4. De Certeau: Hammel

A5. Genette: Geographic achrony

B1-13. Barthes: *S/Z*

C1. Cohn: Narrated Monologue

C2. Chatman: Voice

C3. Mazza: Point of View

C4. Thornton: Showing

C5. Lakoff: Narrative and Society

C6. Todorov: Narrator > Character

C7. Mazza: Allen

C8. Reagan et al.: Person

D1. Chynoweth: Gender

D2. Lakoff: E-mail

A1.

Every day at work Amy would go through the same routine. For the first five hours she would attend diligently and cheerfully to the tasks at hand: answering phones, making calls, and keeping her boss's appointment book updated. During the sixth hour, her pace would decelerate, unfinished projects would reach stopping places, dockets would go back into filing cabinets, and the stapler would return to the drawer. Then for the next half hour she would continue to answer the phone while she made notes to herself of images, metaphors, puns, rhymes, palindromes, the unusual spelling of a client's name—anything that had occurred to her throughout the day. Then came 4:15—afternoon breaktime and the single Eve Light 120 cigarette her perfectly flawed discipline allowed, savored at a concrete breakroom table beside humming vending machines in a gigantic warehouse filled with palettes and stacks of magazines. Amy would spend the final half hour of work, during which her boss talked on the phone with her husband and child, using the company's computer to write and laser-print the following poem:

the inefficient appearance of efficiency

> when the expediter smiles
> and gently reels in her leash
> her assistant scatters files
> and drops a stack of microfiche
>
> when the coordinator happens by
> the conversation freezes
> we all twitch busily under her eye
> and wait until breaktime for sneezes
>
> when the director stalks the halls
> the directed speed to a frenzied blur
> when the supervisor calls
> everyone races to answer her
>
> when the hour is five at night
> the sun expires in citrus light
> we slip on our coats and file our fright
> it's quite a quite a sight
>
> when the hour is eight you see
> us boast goodmorning pointedly
> though nobody smiles we all agree
> it's something to something to see

She would understand that this poem suffered from the fact that she spent so little time on it ("Ballad of the Copyright Clearance Coordinator"—a full page—had been typed in a minute) but she didn't want to get fired. She wondered whether Dominique would consider that a "constraint" and briefly imagined saying something direct to Dominique about art, tongue like a whip, cracking the frosted glass between them.

A1. Genette: Iterative

My score implies that events in my story will happen sequentially. Gerard Genette suggests only alternatives:

I.   Order: sequence of events

      A.   story: the events as they are told

      B.   history: the events (of the story) before they were told[1]

      C.   anachronism: discrepancy between story and historical sequence

            1.   external anachronisms: scenes which refer to events outside (before or after) the history

            2.   internal anachronisms: scenes which refer (out of sequence) to events inside (during) the history

                a)   completive anachronisms: scenes which fill in a previous or later ellipses in the story

                b)   repetitive anachronisms: scenes which repeat a historical period

                    (1)   announcements (anticipations): foreshadowing, a scene which refers to a scene that hasn't happened yet

                    (2)   recalls (retrospections): flashbacks, scenes which refer to a scene that happened earlier

                    (3)   anticipations within retrospections: flashforward within flashback

                c)   retrospections within anticipations: flashback within flashforward

      D.   achronism: scenes which are organized without chronology

II.   Duration: length of scenes relative to the amount of historical time

      A.   summary: short scene narrating long period of history

      B.   scene: when story and historical time are supposed to be nearly equal

      C.   stasis: when the story progresses although historical time is at a standstill

      D.   ellipsis: historical time omitted from the story

III.   Frequency: "relative frequency of the narrated events and the narrative sections that report them" (6)

      A.   singulative: one scene narrates one historical period

      B.   repetitive: "story-repetitions exceed in number the number of events"

      C.   iterative: one scene narrates "several recurrences of the same event or, to be more precise, of several analogical events considered only by respect to what they have in common" (7)

            1.   internal iteration: an iteration within a singulative scene summarizing things which repeat within the historical period narrated by the scene

            2.   external iteration: an iteration within a singulative scene summarizing repetitions from outside the historical period narrated by the scene

      D.   pseudoiteration: an iteration whose precision makes its repetition implausible ("Order")

---

1.   It is worth stressing here that "history" does not mean history. "History" refers to a bounded segment of fictional time, the segment of time the story is concerned with. There are many events outside "history," including fictional experiences the characters had before and after the period of time bounded by the story and its "history."

At 4:45, remembering Dominique's enthusiasm for her "minimum wage poetry," she would consider calling her thesis advisor and leaving a voice mail message saying that she had changed her mind: her thesis was going to be a collection of poetry entitled "Steal Poetry from Work." But it seemed as though this semester there was an unusually high number of Master's candidates writing books of poetry for their final theses. Dominique was working on a collection of poetry entitled "Table of Forms" that Amy didn't have the nerve to ask her about. Afraid of being evaluated on poetry (whose rules were unclear (even proper grammar was unnecessary) and whose conventions (or lack thereof) were flexible (why is prose poetry poetry?)) — she ended up forgetting the call, her degree, and her thesis, which was due in a month, for which she had written a hasty proposal — something her advisor had suggested about the panopticon and *Don Quixote*. She realized she had burned out and could no longer read through the smoke.

She found herself picking up more and more hours. What was supposed to be a parttime assistantship photocopying course materials had turned into a fifty-or-so-hour-a-week commitment to an office she wasn't even sure could run without her. She reminded her boss of this around five. They agreed she should take some time off.

Iteration struck me as a useful technique to narrate a routine day at a tedious job.[2]

Pseudoiteration is iteration carried to its illogical extreme: it is implied that Amy writes exactly the same poem every day.[3]

---

2   RS—Representation of tedium through the iterative is, incidentally, a favorite device of Flaubert. I also notice interesting things going on with the duration of A1: a radical slowing down from 5 hours that pass in a sentence to a half hour that takes the rest of the page.

3   For examples of internal, external, and pseudo-iterations, consider the following three sentences from R.M. Berry's "Metempsychosis": "And so Dougherty won't play for us after all, won't practice the Chaconne this evening, won't feel his thumb cramp, won't ever become anything more than he is despite the accumulated momentum of this rage, his restless nights, all the unplayed music he has somehow managed to hear. Or maybe because of those things. He slumps down into his chair and tries hard not to imagine what he'll be forced to say before this episode mercifully concludes, all the grim faces he'll have to forget, the sweaty rooms he'll pass through, for he's about to realize what he's been trying not to know for the length of this whole story, for twenty-two years now, for as long as you and I have been struggling to protect the last remnants of our own childhood, about to realize that standing beside the chiffonier staring up at the stars that make no music, that rising like this each night believing the sounds in his head were so massive they had long since crushed his heart, that all this time he's never once heard repeated what Segovia played for fifteen-year-old him and five thousand others, what Bach wrote and Mendelssohn, Schumann, Willhelm, Hermann, Brahms, Raff, Busoni rearranged, what Anaheim had tried to teach him not to mangle beyond recognition, that the reason he never sharps the C every afternoon is because he never hears it sharp, because he doesn't want to hear it sharp, because what if he did and it was just music? about to confront this most perverse species of human folly, the plain fact that nothing makes him hornier than the possibility of his own death, and so will end up here with his left elbow hooked over the bed, his legs spread out over a scramble of sheet music and guitar chords, surrounded by strangers who want to hurt him, having been given the chance to love the world or be crushed by it and furiously, achingly, terrifyingly conscious now that he chose the latter because he found annihilation imaginable whereas love has become for him something infinitely strange." (66–67) [RS—This is a fascinating example, but needs analysis.]

A2.

Though she was the most attentive lover Amy had ever had, Dominique did not realize that her confidence as a writer was intimidating. When Amy went over to her apartment after work, Dominique pretended as though she hadn't been writing all afternoon, but Amy could tell by the ashtray she had. Amy was jealous both of Dominique's ability to work and the way she could make it conspicuous by trying to hide it. Amy couldn't write poetry alone. Even when she was alone, especially when she was alone, there was a crowd of voices reading every line she put down. Even when she tried to read, the eyes of all the people who had read it before her were now turned to her, anticipating her response, and she would stiffen, ignore the passages that appealed to her, and dwell on the sentences that had been underlined by the person who had owned the book before her. She had to read in crowded, loud, impossible coffeeshops, because she could not read without witnesses. While she had begun the semester happy to be reading lots of narratology for the first time and becoming visible in the world of discourse her friends inhabited, she began to suspect that everything she said was wrong, and she quickly began to focus on the aspects of the text other people saw. At this point, she found it helpful to read (secondary) criticism about (primary) criticism to familiarize herself with the way the (primary) criticism was normally discussed. She made conscious efforts to copy the way Becka or Dominique acted in the seminar. She tried to look as though she wasn't trying to look as though she were interested. She longed for desks in rows and tests that required #2 pencils. She longed for cheerleading squad locker rooms. She longed for mononucleosis. She longed to get out of academia and the competition for a handful of faculty positions in which, ultimately, she would be denied tenure.

But Dominique. This kept her just outside the circle of discourse in which Dominique's precise speaking and writing shone through the murk of translated theory. Amy became trapped, became unable to talk to the other students, and found herself locked in a spire of Dominique's heart on the perimeter of a patriarchal castle of understanding, glittering and magnificent, full of staircases and categories and hallways and metaphors and secret passages and narratives and cathedrals and schemata and cellars and metonymy and women locked in various masters' bedrooms all staring at her through the bars of distant windows across a textless abyss. Amy might become another woman's wife and lean forever on a vodka and gaze out across the mosaic-tiled commons she would never wander again. Monogamy, a square in the mosaic, suggested a grid in the confused tangle of pieces from different jigsaw puzzles. Without a constant friend, she was afraid of being put back in a puzzle box, alone, and ending up lying in the darkness staring at the invisible rules printed underneath the lid. The world wanted her only to be on time and balance her checkbook. Dominique wanted her to do the inexplicable: to slide into the infinity between the lines of a text, to find the fusebox in an underground maze of mirrors using only the light of a single match, to fight for scraps of meaning in the howling blackness between the sign and the rest of us, to evaporate into theory and expand to connect all of time and space and text, to assume confidence and let competence follow, to grow a tie. There would never again be a Dominique who loved Amy. Any other Dominique would love somebody else, someone with pencils sharp enough to carve haiku on the head of a pin, novels on diamonds, a Masters thesis on the first period of *To the Lighthouse*; somebody who could make shadowpuppets in a laser beam, who could talk Kristeva with Dominique, eyes flashing.

A2. Lakoff: Character and Metaphor

What is a character? Shlomith Rimmon-Kenan identifies two pairs of opposed definitions: semiotic vs. mimetic, and actor vs. action (31-36). A semiotic character is a linguistic construction, whereas a mimetic character represents a real person.[4] Aristotle, Propp, and Greimas are among those who "reduce" or "subordinate" characters to action (34). Conversely, Ferrara considers character to be the central "structuring element" of fiction (35). Roland Barthes, between 1966 and 1970, seems to move from the first position towards the latter without ever getting there.[5] For my purposes these distinctions are not useful as blanket statements about which aspects of character are reductions of or subordinate to the others. I consider these assumed dichotomies an interesting classification scheme. Most characters are all four things: a linguistic construction representing a person whose actions are important. Different aspects of character are privileged in different stories and even by different characters within a single story. I once wrote a story narrated by a dinner plate—which is neither a person nor capable of action, though it is personified through interior monologue and acted upon.

In this story I propose a new definition of character: a metaphor system. To explain this, I will have to explain what I mean by metaphor. My definition is adapted from the contemporary theory of metaphor as articulated by Lakoff et al.

---

4   But is character as 'dead' as all that? Do the new views dispense with it altogether, or do they only dismantle a certain traditional concept of it? (31)

5   RS—It would be instructive to speculate here about how Ferrara and Barthes might read A2.

Dominique using a cigarette as a crutch; building a crystalline empire of thought on a stone ashtray.

Dominique, from inside whose heart Amy could see only murky, filtered daylight; felt exposed to Amy's attention.

Dominique, who would obtain the last tenuretrack position in the world; and consider it an interesting exercise.

Dominique, who felt deflated whenever other writers used the ideas she explained to them clearly; was the fifth color in the map of their friends.

Dominique, which was a pseudonym for an opaque bubble of secret identities.

Dominique, who talked Amy into quitting her job, moving in with her, spending spring break in the library, finishing their theses, getting Masters Degrees in English, and leaving Austen State University and Illinois forever. Dominique had a lot of money, so Amy found herself without a reason to continue working at Instructional Copying.

Dominique's birthday occurred two days after Amy's last day at work just as a thunderstorm began while Amy was carrying the last box of books—a box labeled "Not the Canon"—up the three flights. The present Amy gave her was a book of poetry by Carolyn Forche. The card Amy made her was a collage of photographs of their friends. Each image was torn from a different photograph, with deliberately haphazard rips and tears, and parts of the photographs were spotted with bleach, other parts sanded. The photograph of herself was a smaller scale version of the technique used to make the entire collage, a patchwork torn from different photographs of her.

Dominique's mother called to wish her a happy birthday and made her copy down an extremely long poetry assignment (Jean Arp: Konfiguration Poems). During the phone call, the power disappeared in a crash of lightning, and the call was terminated. Both Amy and Dominique were relieved by this. They lit candles. Amy talked Dominique into getting drunk—she always appreciated that. Dominique suggested they get as drunk and giddy as possible drinking only milkshakes, milkshakes laced with Baileys Irish Cream, coffee, Kahlua, chocolate syrup, Tia Maria, malt powder, Amaretto, Sheridans, Godiva, espresso... All of which Dominique actually had in her well-stocked kitchen.

They filled a bathtub with the last hot water in the building and basil oil.

Amy and Dominique agreed to be monogamous for awhile.

Outside the bathroom window three flights down a man with a wooden leg was pacing near the corner streetlamp in the rain.

Eventually another man came and they walked away together.

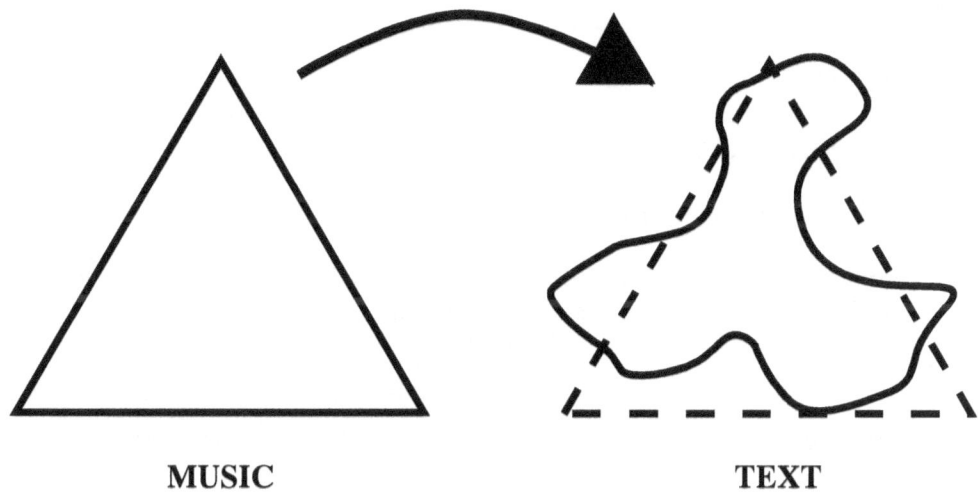

MUSIC   TEXT

Barthes's Metaphor: Text is Music

Source Domain: Music

Target Domain: Text

Mapping: A musical score and a musical performance map simultaneously onto text, with composers and performers mapping simultaneously onto writers.

Revealed (qualities music and text share): Music and text are both written, both art, and both involve sequence.

Concealed (qualities text has that music does not):
The rate at which a text is read is controlled by the reader.

Illusion (qualities music has that text does not):
Music can be divided into equal metronomic intervals.
Musical notation involves simultaneity.

DIAGRAM 2

This diagram is a model of metaphor. The diagram shows a triangle being superimposed on (mapped onto) a blob. In the process, certain parts of the blob are revealed: where the triangle and blob overlap. Certain parts of the blob are concealed: the parts of the blob the triangle does not overlap. The parts of the triangle that do not overlap the blob create an illusion: the illusion that there is blob there. This model can be thought of as a specific metaphor for the general process of metaphor. This diagram is the source domain and the general process of metaphor is the target domain. This model reveals that a metaphor will reveal certain

A3.

"You're late."

"I'm paying good money to be late too."

"Do you have anything you'd like to tell me?"

"I've been living in denial. Denial of the fact that I'm a graduate student. Denial, also, of the fact that at some *level*, I love text. I've been pretending I'm normal. I quit my job almost a week ago. I'm afraid my boss feels betrayed. I feel like I lost a friend. How's that."

"Fine. Your *boss*?"

"She's a real friendly African American woman, very physically affectionate, compliments my outfits, likes to joke about getting high during lunch. She used to make me nervous, being so personal, always behind the one-way glass of her office. I'm hardly conservative, but I don't get jobs because I need friends, usually. I don't mind women being physically affectionate with me but I felt I had no choice. I felt like she was taking advantage of the fact that she had the eyes, and only she could look the other way. One day I saw her supervisor chew her out because her supervisor had been listening in on one of her phone conversations with a client—an economics professor who was mad because his course packet wasn't finished on time who said something rude and made my boss furious; then I felt less nervous about the fact that she was always inspecting me. Some weird mixture of love and control. I knew that she could monitor my computer screen so I started writing poems about work. Some weird mixture of love and... resistance, I guess. And then I found I could write again. The risk was not that the poetry might go unnoticed and uncommented upon, like in a workshop."

"You mean the *risk* of getting caught."

"No, yeah, no, more like in the certainty of getting caught. I didn't know if she was monitoring me or not, so I had to assume she was. And then... the sense of audience was great. I was acutely aware of an authoritative reader reading every word as I *wrote* it. So even the composition became a performance, in a way. Even though the poems were premeditated—I took lots of notes beforehand—I had to write them without revision. I had to pretend that they just came to involuntarily, a spasm of brilliance, a mystical process involving muses and creative forces more powerful than the workplace. That way it wouldn't be my fault that I wrote the poem."

"Is writing poetry like that for you?"

"Shit no. It's not like that for anybody. You should have seen Dominique last night. She had two dictionaries and a set of Scrabble letters she kept arranging on the tabletop. Writing Twenty Consonant Poetry. It took her an hour just to write a single line. No. Forget what you read in college, doc. Maybe Jack Kerouac can eat Benzedrine and write a novel in a day (with his mom to cook for him). Maybe Allen Ginsberg can eat

aspects of its target domain, conceal others, and imply certain illusory qualities of the target domain. This model creates the illusion that metaphor involves superimposing the source domain onto the target domain and conceals the fact that mapping involves creating correspondences between aspects of the source and target domain. [6]

I created characters by mapping the metaphor systems they think, speak, and live by. I attempted to engineer conflict between the characters by giving them conflicting metaphor systems—incompatible world views.[7] Here is the score of the four characters' metaphor systems:

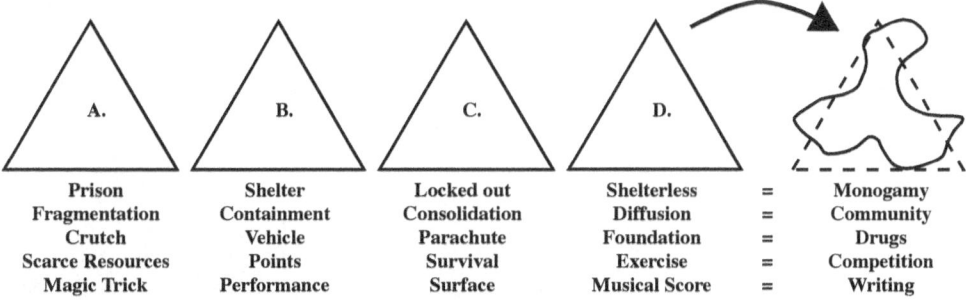

Prison	Shelter	Locked out	Shelterless	=	Monogamy
Fragmentation	Containment	Consolidation	Diffusion	=	Community
Crutch	Vehicle	Parachute	Foundation	=	Drugs
Scarce Resources	Points	Survival	Exercise	=	Competition
Magic Trick	Performance	Surface	Musical Score	=	Writing

DIAGRAM 3

This shows the metaphor systems for the four characters. The same target domains (blobs) are understood in terms of different, sometimes contradictory, source domains (triangles).

---

6   This diagram is best explained with a narrative: Pythagoras has been wandering alone in the desert for weeks. He is nearly dead from thirst when he sees a gigantic shimmering blob. He does not understand it. It resembles a triangle, however, and he understands triangles quite well. He knows that triangles are defined by any three nonlinear points, their area is equal to half their base times their height, the sum of their angles is 180 degrees, in the case of right triangles the square of the hypotenuse is equal to the sum of the squares of the two other sides, and so on. While none of this describes the blob, the triangle is a useful model. Pythagoras begins to understand the blob as a triangle, and, in so doing, gains a certain understanding of it (the overlap between triangle and blob (the revealed)), acquires certain illusions (represented by the parts of the triangle that fall outside the blob (the illusory)), and loses sight of certain features of the blob (the parts of the blob that fall outside the triangle (the concealed)). [RS—But is the shimmering blob water? Or a mirage?]

7   RS—One of the theoretical problems I find running throughout your essay is a conflation of metaphor and narrative. Are there significant differences that we should be noting between the two? Between, for example, the instantaeous, static nature of metaphor and the temporal, progressive nature of narrative?

mescaline and channel Blake and bang out an eight page hallucination that ends up in *The Norton Anthology of Modern Poetry* but it isn't like that really. Ever see the draft of "The Waste Land" that Eliot got back from Pound with whole pages crossed out? Ever read "The Philosophy of Composition" by Edgar Allen Poe?"

"Which?"

"You'd like it. Anyway, the language is dead. If there's anything that hasn't been written, it must be pretty long. Dominique will write it I'm sure."

"Do you feel as though you are competing with your friends?"

"No. I mean, I was, but I lost."

"*Lost?*"

"The survival of the fittest. I have genetically weak eye muscles. I can't read as quickly as predators."

"*Can't.*"

"Not like I'm supposed to. I can't pay attention. Unless I feel the author is addressing me, feel like the author is listening to me, waiting to hear me respond. That's rare though. Usually, the author is speaking a different language, and that's *my* fault, usually French. Ever read Michel DeCerteau?"

"I'm afraid I don't know who that is."

"You'd like him. Ever read Bakhtin?"

"I'm afraid that as a doctor my liberal arts background is somewhat weak."

"That was polite. I hear voices when I write."

"*Voices?*"

"Well, maybe *voices* isn't the right word. No, never mind, it's the right word."

"Whose *voices?*"

"Other writers, my father, my friends, definitely Mr. Chrzastowski."

"Who?"

"My thesis advisor. He's read everything."

"How do you spell *Chrzastowski?*"

A3. Genette: Proust

A story, Genette implies, can be only permutations of its history. One can look only for ratios between periods of time in the history and amount of narrative. I wrote part A of the story to demonstrate aspects of Genette's descriptions of story time. I used his structural descriptions of Proust's *A la recherche du temps perdu*. Barthes' metaphor implies that my story is Proust transcribed by ear and played back by another composer/performer. I have never read Proust's *A la recherche du temps perdu*

> It could be roughly summarized by stressing, on the one hand, the gradual slowing down of the narrative by the insertion of longer and longer scenes for events of shorter and shorter duration. This is compensated for, on the one hand, by the presence of more and more extensive ellipses. ("Order" page unknown)

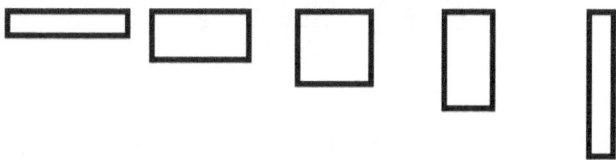

DIAGRAM 4

As before, the story moves through time from left to right. Each rectangle is a scene. The width of the rectangles indicates how much story time they cover, the height of the rectangles indicates how long the scene lasts. The gaps between the rectangles indicate increasingly long ellipses: unnarrated periods of historical time.

One of the most interesting ways music and text are dissimilar is that music unfolds in time and stories unfold in sequence.[8] A conventional orchestral tonal musical score indicates precise durations. It is possible for a composer to structure the parameter of time very exactly. Music is written in equal metronomic intervals. It has a basic chronological unit: the measure. In the case of a written story, the rate at which the story will be read will be controlled by the reader. There are numerous ways the author can indicate tempo and rhythm. Saunders writes that our experience of time in a novel—tempo and pace—is a function of rhythm. One of the elements of textual rhythm Saunders proposes is the

8   RS—I'm not sure what the difference is between "unfolding in time" and "unfolding in sequence." Can you clarify? WG—Music is in real time. A proper performance of Strauss's *Don Quixote* should always last three quarters of an hour, whereas it is unlikely that any two readings of Cervantes will last the same amount of time—it is the sequence of events in the book that is important, not the duration of reading.

"Fake it."

"You haven't mentioned your father very much."

"When I was a kid, my dad was in jail. He was busted for possession. Mom and I went to visit him every weekend. I hated him. I tried to turn my mother against him but she kept going. What I hated most was how safe he seemed there. He always complained, but I could only think of all the things my mother had to deal with everyday. When I was sixteen I managed to convince her to let me stay home and I started having sex. I saw my father only a couple of times after that. At the time I swore I would never marry or even love. I would never have believed I'd be this close to Dominique now."

"You evidently care about her a great deal."

"*Evidently*. One of the first poems she sent me was a rebus... can I see your pen? Sure, hide your notes from me, fine. Thanks. Here:

I didn't understand it as a rebus. She had to explain it to me, just like the palindrome, just like the acrostic. I read it as eye, heart, smile; meaning love, observation, and patience. Analyze **that**. She's my witness. She's my shrink. I come here because there are a few things I can't talk about with her. There are a lot more things I can't talk about with you."

"*Things*?"

"Did you ever read Lacan? Krist- Did they make you guys read Freud?"

"Meter or Measure: the stasis against which movement is related, compared, or varied; it is the 'something standing still' against which movement can be perceived and measured…" (2) What is the basic unit of text? Is it textual: the page, paragraph, sentence, word, or letter; is it phonological: the phoneme or syllable (as in metric or rhyming poetry); or is it semantic: a unit of meaning (as in Barthes' lexias)? Can we measure a text in metaphors?

Genette writes of a discrepancy between history time and story time without implying that the two can ever synch up. He gives us a set of discrepancies without ever alluding to the possibility that a story can show its history in "real time."

> Generally speaking, the idea of an isochrony between narrative and "history" is highly ambiguous, for the narrative unit which, in literature, is almost always a narrative text cannot really be said to possess a definite duration. One could equate the time of a narrative with the time it takes to read it, but reading-times vary considerably from reader to reader, and an ideal average speed can only be determined by fictional means. It may be better to start out from a definition in the form of a relative quantity, and define isochrony as a uniform projection of historical time onto narrative extension, that is, number of pages per duration of event." ("Order, Duration, and Frequency")

A story, Genette implies, can only be permutations of its history. One can only look for ratios between periods of time in the history and number of pages (the unit he proposes as well as the unit I have chosen to work with) in the story.

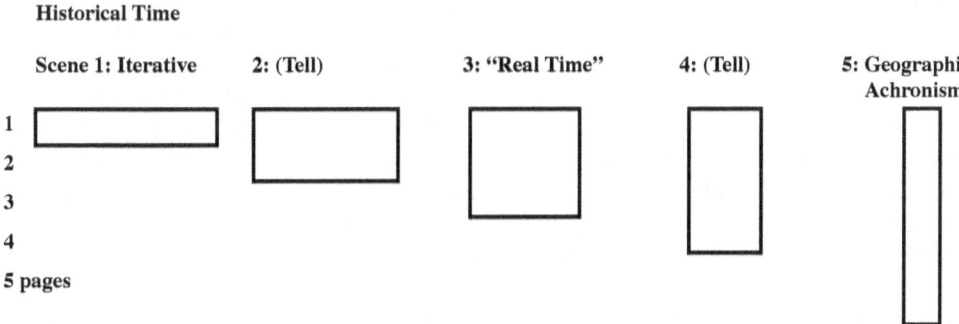

DIAGRAM 5

This shows the same shape—A1–5—with brief descriptions of how scenes 1-4 are to written.

A4.

But Dominique. On a trip to Chicago made with no more deliberation than Dominique saying "grab your coat I want to take you to see Thirty Plays in Sixty Minutes," through an exaggerated performance of reading to Amy a poem aloud, Dominique, raised copy of May Swenson's *In Other Words* in her left hand, her right arm around Amy's waist and beneath her skirt, on the train, amid other passengers, brought Amy to orgasm so slowly and precisely that Amy's gasp, when it came, might have been a sigh of appreciation for the poem itself.

It had been a week since they stayed in the bathtub for two days, adding more warm water every few hours, making occasional overland treks to the refrigerator, and talking inexhaustibly.

Amy felt the glances of the other passengers get tangled in her hair. The thought that Amtrak might be watching made her wonderfully aroused. She felt conspicuous when she was with Dominique anywhere. Dominique was used to being conspicuous. Getting away with more than she suspected they were suspected of getting away with defused all her fear. Outside the window, quiet flat farmland panned by. The rumbling of the tracks tickled Amy's tingling feet, and she sank close as Dominique read the final stanza.

> "So get me out of jail!"
> "Of course." Applying my picklock nail
> to the latch, I freed her. (103)

(In the bathtub Amy had complained: "Being an English major is like being stupid. All the time. Whether you're trying to read Judith Butler or listening to the mechanic tell you what's wrong with your car. You're from another planet, you understand time and money and text differently than normal people. My boss could never figure out that I was reading course packets the whole time. She thought I did really good quality checks because I read every word. She made weird jokes: as if I came to work high, or spaced out, or stole office supplies, or goofed off. For all her Total Quality Management training, she couldn't figure out that I was reading on the job, reading Marx and Weber, reading entire course packets for Cultural Studies or Urban Planning or Political Science, occasionally remastering really good articles and then retrieving the old masters from the recycling bin to take home. One day I was checking this film studies packet and I was reading "Art in the Age of Mechanical Reproduction" and I couldn't believe how funny it was to me, writing poetry on the sly at my copy center job, and I started laughing. The boss came out of her office and really wanted to know what the joke was and I couldn't explain it to her. I had to tell her it was a private thought so she could assume it was something lewd, maybe having to do with the word "Reproduction."")

Dominique had rubbed so much peppermint soap on Amy's back that it burned. "I envy you. You read a lot."

"So do you."

"I can't read—I write too much."

In A3, I explore exactly this questionable idea of "real time." "Real time" in film would be any unedited single take replayed forwards at the same speed: the amount of time that passes in the scene is the same as the amount of time it takes to watch. In a story, "real time" indicates that the amount of story time that passes in the scene is somehow equivalent to the amount of historical time covered by the scene. My solution to the problem of writing a scene in "real time" is to write a scene entirely in dialogue. This solution will exclude the narrative stasis inherent in narration: every word will play itself out in story time and historical time simultaneously. I have adapted this idea from David Foster Wallace's *The Broom of the System* in which certain scenes are written entirely in what he calls "unattributed dialogue." While unattributed dialogue is disorienting for the reader, for the writer it provides a way to avoid coming up with synonyms for "said." It was only after I had written A3 that I realized that some of the unattributed dialogue in *The Broom of the System* is between central characters and a psychoanalyst. I found this unintended coincidence unfortunate. He didn't think much of it: he finds the psychoanalyst a convenient way to "triangulate" a character. To facilitate the reader's ability to decipher the scene, I intentionally made the psychoanalyst's lines as "contrived" (JH) as possible. The psychoanalyst who appears in A3 does not recur. He (she)[9] is an invisible unnarrated and flat[10] character. The psychoanalyst is an example of a character whose presence is more semiotic than mimetic, whose actions are superordinate and whose identity is subordinate.[11] My intention is writing this scene as a psychoanalysis session was to attribute Amy's personality to her formative experiences. This is circuitously Freudian. Having defined Amy's personality as an unconscious (in Lakoff's sense, not Freud's) metaphor system, I then tried to ground her source domains in her childhood experiences.[12] The psychoanalysis session only serves to underline this strategy: Amy's childhood experiences could have been indicated any number of ways. Although I made no effort to write this scene convincingly or well, the idea remains as a possible model of character, possibly even personality.

A3, unnarrated, is the first of many attempts I make throughout the story to distinguish "showing" from "telling." I propose that unattributed dialogue is (paradoxically?) the purest form of "showing."

---

9   KD—"Is this doctor a man or a woman? I think I want it to be a woman, but it sounds like a man. Specifically, I can't say why though."

10   SF—"2D"

11   RS—A "foil" in literary terms?

12   RS—Though the recent past seems to govern her behavior far more than the distant past; in other words, I guess I wasn't terribly convinced by the "source domains in childhood experiences."

"Bitch."

"No splashing! Hey!"

"You have enraged me. I dump the shampoo on you."

"Stop. I'm warning you, you dadburned varmint. I'll lick yer hide."

"Sensor overload: tongue in sector seven. Activate shampoo field. Beep."

"Oh dear, I seem to have become beshampooed by an unusual space alien. Quite."

"Rather."

"Heavens. We must freshen the water now. I'm so glad those... *workers* managed to restore the power."

"Indeed."

"I shall, however, be ready for their revolution after our bath."

"Yes. Which scientists predict should coincide with the discovery in the year 2000 that the Earth is actually Venus, and has been all along."

"Hey, remember how I was trying to explain that essay to you?"

"That wasn't me. That was my twin sister."

"Okay: in this tub, which is a bounded space thought to be reality-"

"Says who?"

"Aristotle's wife. Anyway, in this tub, we are solid, the water is fluid. Think of us as men–"

"No."

"-and the water as women."

"I see. So everytime the bathwater starts to get discolored, learned, articulate, tries to write something, we pull the plug. Like so: and there you have it, gentlemen. Language is a false idealization of the inexplicable."

"What? That sounds like a dismissal. There may be language, but there are bodies. Which are full of weird fluids, by the way. See?"

"Yuk!")

A4. De Certeau: Hammel

Amy can't read or write without witnesses. In a way, this reflects her metaphor system in which she understands writing in terms of magic tricks. Magic tricks (as opposed to magic) are intended to deceive and impress an audience and are pointless without one: the magician is neither deceived nor impressed by her own sleight of hand. Amy is having trouble with her graduate studies because most of the work of a graduate student—reading and writing—is invisible work done in private. More strongly, though, Amy's condition is an exploration of the ideas in Michel De Certeau's *The Practice of Everyday Life* and our classroom discussion of it. Amy is able to function quite well at her job because she is always visible.[13] Her daily attempts to write poetry at work without being punished by her boss consist of a mixture of sleight of hand—writing when her boss's back is turned—and the smooth unerring confidence of a magician. De Certeau uses "space" and "place" more to distinguish between two different relations to power than two different types of physical locations. A workplace is a "place"—it is organized and governed by an occupying power structure. A "space"—which can be a transformation of a "place"—is a position of calculated resistance against the power structure. An apartment is the landlord's "place," but a "space" for the tenant. De Certeau also distinguishes between "strategies" and "tactics." "Strategies" are strategies of the power structure—the fact that everything Amy types can be seen by her boss, should her boss choose to observe Amy to make sure she is working. "Tactics," conversely, are acts of resistance. De Certeau describes them as "a maneuver within the enemy's field of vision" and "an art of the weak." (37) Amy steals poetry from work as a "tactic." De Certeau's ideas are adapted from Foucault's discussion of the panopticon, and Amy's workplace is an adaptation of (our classroom discussion of) De Certeau's adaptation. Chambers on de Certeau: "A paradigmatic case of oppositional behavior is the practice of 'ripping off,' called *la perruque* in French factories" (*Room* 6). This is a view of work which is not motivated by profit.[14]

---

13   RS—I think you could do a lot more here (and in other sections) with the concept of the gaze: which can be intrusive or erotic (voyeurism), a mechanism of power (panopticism), a vehicle of/for desire (revelation), etc.

14   RS—Or perhaps motivated by an alternative notion of "profit"—one that benefits immediately, locally, that can't be saved or reinvested, that flows to the source of labor rather than the capitalist.

On the train, half asleep, Amy felt the other passengers' intentions stretch ahead down tracks parallel to her own. In this alignment she found herself compatible with people who would otherwise appear to her as jagged shards to avoid. In rows their angles fell into a perfect tangram. The passengers ahead of her were not in her way. They would all reach their destination together, or not at all. Dominique continued reading to herself in the silence of an erased history.

(They had almost no models to understand their attraction to each other. It was the opposite of what Amy's role at work had been: clearly defined and not meant to fit her. It was the desk's job, and she was the desk's latest assistant. The standard procedures for her position (Typing Clerk III) was outlined on a laminated sheet somewhere in the bottom drawer. It was there to refer to the very moment the boss should have a short and angry talk with her husband and come storming out flashing violent eyes at Amy, who would quickly stop composing, click on another window and resume some task exactly as if she had been working steadily all afternoon, even at 5:01 on her last day. At 5:15 they were making daiquiris in the paper shredder. At 6:30 they were smoking marijuana on the roof of the building. Her boss put her head on Amy's shoulder and told her that she would miss reading Amy's poems every day.)

(Amy told her therapist this and then (she liked to wait until her hour was almost over before saying what was really bothering her, talking about sex, forcing her curious therapist to delay his next appointment) about how she imagined that if she found Dominique with another lover she'd freak, especially if it were a man. Once, when Dominique came home late, Amy had imagined her with Becka, which was unlikely, but she escaped into a detailed fantasy in which the eye in Dominique's heart was a mirror and Amy went behind it and found a roomful of monitors and compared her image with the others as shown on surveillance cameras. She turned the mirrors to the wall, pulled the blinds, and refused to answer the phone, until, on the machine, she heard Dominique calling to ask for a ride home.)

De Certeau seems to propose the narrative as a substitute for, or a supplement to, "cut out" and "invert" theory.

> A *possibility* offers itself for making explicit the relation of theory to the procedures from which it results and to those which are its objects: a discourse composed of stories.... In many works, narrativity insinuates itself into scientific discourse as its general denomination (its title), as one of its parts ("case" studies, "life stories," or stories of groups, etc.) or as its counterpoint (quoted fragments, interviews, "sayings," etc.). Narrativity haunts such discourse. Shouldn't we recognize its scientific legitimacy by assuming that instead of being a remainder that cannot be, or has not yet been, eliminated from discourse, narrativity has a necessary function in it, and that *a theory of narration is indissociable from a theory of practices, as its condition as well as its production?* (78)

I am better able to advance an abstract argument through fiction than I am through an essay. This essay is distorting my knowledge by eliding my ignorances. I am writing in an omniscient disembodied voice of feigned objectivity and universality.[15] The story is spoken through a character assumed to be idiosyncratic, if not completely unreliable. It is clear that the story is narrated by a person who is deliberately concealing their stake in it. The ideas lose their claim to truth, and, through conflicts between characters, alternative ideas can exist in dynamic counterpoint. The story offers me opportunities to explore ideas that the essay impedes. The fact of the narrative insists that I relate the ideas to people.

In trying to represent theoretical ideas in this story, subtly and overtly, on structural, metaphoric and narrative "levels," I received a great deal of criticism from the only member of the workshop who admits to being committed to theory:

> The primary question we have to discuss... is whether there is an accountable difference between "literary" fiction and fiction that acts as a diegetic exercise. Yours is the latter, it seems to me (if this latter exists), a piece whose function is to explicate and re-embody ideas whose original texts are not engaged in their *primary* forms. That is, your story serves to empty the content of one form into another, to siphon Irigaray from "This Sex Which is not One" into a scene with two lovers splashing each other in a tub. The motive behind such

A5.

The last ray of the setting sun is coming down Luxembourg Avenue and into the main library building. It reflects off somebody's goldplated digital watch and past the chair near the Circulation desk where, twenty minutes earlier, Dominique found Amy half into a coma staring through tears at reams of printouts. Amy had, after a week of (admittedly sporadic) research, concluded that there was no English translation of *Don Quixote* available at the University library. Her search had yielded such a bewildering proliferation of secondary sources that it had taken her three days to sort through the items on the computer (very few of which were at the their proper place on the shelves), read many, turn aside many more...

>
> ...25. TITLE: The Inedible Text
> AUTHOR: Esquival-Bonati, Laura
>
> 26. TITLE: Objectivity of the subject: narrative reliability in Don Quixote
> AUTHOR: Ziolkowsky, Juergen
>
> 27. TITLE: Implausible dreams
> AUTHOR: Lo Re, Jozef
>
> 28. TITLE: Don Quixote in opera (1680-1876)
> AUTHOR: Aylward, Lisa...

...and conclude that none alone could help her, and that reading them all would be madness. Searches with frustrating databases and embarrassingly competent librarians uncovered books, essays, a story, a different novel with the same title, Cliffs Notes, dread, anxiety, and ulcerous pangs. When Dominique found her, Amy was sitting in the same chair she had sat in Thursday, the day before, when the stacks worker had called out the last two digits of her social security number so that she could come and claim her copy of *Don Quixote*, in *Russian*.

It ricochets off the brass vacuum tubes and out a window on the south side of the building, angling over the steps of Walker Hall where, Thursday, suddenly dizzy, Amy had had to sit down, having read the Foucault:

> Having first read so many books that he became a sign, a sign wandering through a world that did not recognize him, he has now, despite himself and without his knowledge, become a book that contains his truth, that records exactly all that he has done and said and seen and thought, and that at last makes him recognizable, so closely does he resemble all those signs whose ineffaceable imprint he has left behind him. (48)

an exercise is itself hermeneutic.[16] We can understand Irigaray in a different way through some "real" images that ostensibly *we all can see*. That assumes that the original text is not "visible" to us all, a point that concerns your character directly. Her struggles in an academic setting provide the motive for your exercise; her inability to access a discourse (see "The Resistance to Theory" Paul de Man) seems to me the reasoning behind providing a different route of *access* to an "inaccessible" idea. What this process assumes is that ideas in Irigaray, or de Certeau, can themselves be "divisible" from their texts and that access is a matter of de(re)contextualization. (JH)

Are de Certeau's ideas separable from his writing? Since I have only read a translation of his writing, either the ideas have been separated from the original text or the ideas are no longer his. This project is built on the assumptions that ideas can be separated from texts and used to create new ones, that the ideas will change, and that the new texts may not noticeably resemble the old ones.[17] My story may remind nobody of Proust. As to whose ideas they are, and as to what constitutes a difference between ideas, I will leave that to Becka and Dominique to work out.

---

16   When I first read this letter I was nowhere near a dictionary and had to give up when I hit the word "hermeneutic." On the following page, he writes: "Often in lit. crit. Discourse, the 'literary' refers to the figural, ambiguous, unknowable reach of language that does not explicitly refer to its referent. It is, in common terms, the 'slippage' of the signifier." That I don't know what he means by "common terms" is a relevant point to this discussion.
17   RS—You seem to be sidestepping the intriguing, if difficult, theoretical issue that you pose for yourself.

It passes a cardinal whose red wings are spread as it descends onto a windowsill, and enters Stein Hall where, Wednesday, when an empty classroom she had appropriated to read in began to fill with students, Amy remained in the back row through an entire history lecture. Reading for the third time "Pierre Menard, Author of Don Quixote," a story by Jorge Luis Borges, whose title alone was confusing. It was about a French writer whose ambition was to write the original *Don Quixote*, word for word, in Spanish, without ever consulting the original, which he had read once. She spent the entire lecture trying to figure out what had seemed strange about the story the first time she read it.

> Every man should be capable of all ideas, and I believe that in the future she will be. (54)

It enters a heating vent and bounces through pipes underground emerging in Dickinson Hall, where, Tuesday, in the atrium where she had first spied on Dominique asleep on a purple sofa, she read the entire Cliffs Notes. Weak with ambivalence, in her notes, she copied down the first sentence:

> *Don Quixote* is a work that has universal and contemporary appeal. (5)

And then the following:

> *Don Quixote* is a work that has universal and contemporary appeal.

> *Don Quixote* is a work that has universal appeal.

> *Don Quixote* is a work that has appeal.

> *Don Quixote* has appeal.

> *Don Quixote* is a work.

> *Don Quixote* works.

It hits somebody's belt buckle and bounces straight up and out the skylight, and, bouncing off an antenna, it passes across a darkening blue sky over the Administration Building where Amy read the Borges story for the second time Monday, after arriving home from Chicago (where Dominique, after the play, had purposefully signaled a cab that took them to an amazing hotel room) just in time to stand in line for half an hour to inquire about the unlikely possibility of dropping a course she hadn't been to in a month. She stood there reading. At first she thought that the narrator was an idiot. She was finding him more and more convincing:

> The text of Cervantes and that of Menard are verbally identical, but the second is almost infinitely richer. (52)

A5.Genette: Geographic Achrony

A4 is structured according to a different part of Genette's analysis of Proust:

$$N(arrative)1 = H(istory)4; N2 = H2; N3 = H4; N4 = H2; N5 = H4... (3)$$

This means that the first scene in the story is the fourth scene in the history ($N1 = H4$). A4 begins in A4, there is a parenthetical flashback to A2, a return to A4, a second flashback to A2, a second return to A4, a flashback to A1, and a flashback to A3.

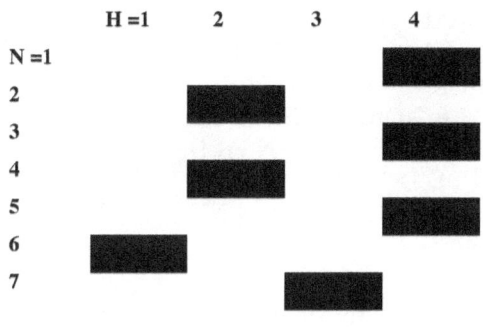

DIAGRAM 6

A4: The beginning of *A la recherche du temps perdu*: the history happens from left to right, the story proceeds from top to bottom.

Of A1–5, according to the earlier diagram, A5 covers the smallest amount of historical time and takes the longest amount of story time (number of pages). A5 takes place almost instantaneously, but, since it consists of a series of flashbacks and a single flashforward, it arguably covers two weeks. A5 tracks through space from location to location, relating salient events that took place in each location up until that moment of historical time.[18]

Genette uses the term "achrony" to indicate stories in which the historical scenes are organized according to criteria which are not chronological. I can think of two types of achrony, which I will call "stasis" (borrowing Genette's term) and "geographic achrony." Stasis refers to a scene or narrative in which no time passes. One might say that this is the case of much of Ambrose Bierce's "An Occurrence at Owl Creek Bridge," in which a deceptively small amount of time passes. A more precise example of stasis can be found in Italo Calvino's "T Zero," a story in which no time passes. Its first sentence:

> I have the impression this isn't the first time I've found myself in this situation: with my bow just slackened in my outstretched left hand, my right hand drawn back, the arrow A suspended in midair at about a third of its trajectory,

18   RS—Spatial organization is a technique favored by Robbe-Grillet

The last ray of sunlight passes through the ivy-laced bell tower above the mathematics library, where, Saturday, Amy, gaining confidence, finished her map of the plot of *Don Quixote* by Kathy Acker (whom she had at first mistaken for a translator), which involved Richard Nixon and a dog. Kathy Acker was spraypainted graffiti worth reading on the sign that wasn't. She now thought of the original Cervantes as a locus of intertextual clichés—as Queneau might say "plagiarism by anticipation." Cervantes, who a week ago was bearer of secrets, who knew everything Amy needed to, was now a Spanish dimestore mannequin robed in lavish French cloth. Cervantes, Cervantes (she scoffed), Cervantes.

> BEING DEAD, DON QUIXOTE
> COULD NO LONGER SPEAK.
> BEING BORN INTO AND PART
> OF A MALE WORLD, SHE HAD
> NO SPEECH OF HER OWN. ALL
> SHE COULD DO WAS READ
> MALE TEXTS WHICH WEREN'T
> HERS. (39)

It, in the Austen State Student Union Bowling Alley, passes through the millimeter gap between a moving bowling ball and a certain strike. The first time she had read "Pierre Menard, Author of Don Quixote," a week earlier, she finished the story, closed the book, put it down, and stared at it for almost a minute as if stung. She really wanted one of the people playing pinball to sense her confusion and come over to the table to she if she was all right, if she needed somebody to explain the story to her, preferably Cervantes, whom she could now easily imagine as a skateboarder with dreadlocks, innocent, hapless, a shrugging scapegoat who could not understand that he had written a great postmodern novel. Somebody bowled a strike and yelled.

> "My undertaking is not essentially difficult... I would only have to be immortal to carry it out." (50)

It wouldn't have been so bad, but she had just read the scene in Paul Auster's *City of Glass* where a character with the same name as the author explains psychotic textual scholarship theories regarding *Don Quixote*, which the character claims was narrated by Sancho Panza to the priest and barber, who had translated it into Arabic, which was the form Cervantes had found it in, before hiring Don Quixote himself to translate it into Spanish.

> But there's one last twist. Don Quixote, in my view, was not really mad. He only pretended to be. (119)

After the poetry reading Friday night, studying with Dominique at the Daily Grind Cafe, halfway through her second cup of confidence, Amy will become wildly decisive: for her thesis, she will write *Don Quixote* (in English), extrapolating from the Cliffs Notes. To do this, she will first become Pierre Menard. Then she will dust the Shklovsky for footnotes, move on to Heine and Turgenev, and plunge into the overpopulated underworld of the intertext. In her notebook she will swiftly write

and, a bit farther on, also suspended in midair, and also at about a third of
its trajectory, the lion L in the act of leaping upon me, jaws agape and claws
extended. (95)

Geographic achrony is a series of scenes arranged according to geographical location,
rather than time.

Events here follow a geographic rather than a chronological pattern. (*Order*
4)

Ian Watt, in his *Rise of the Novel*, describes *Tom Jones* as innovative, because of Fielding's
attempts to tie the scenes of his novel to specific times and places along Tom Jones' route
to London. (23-5) This is an example of a novel arranged according to both geographical
location and time, and is not achronistic as such.

In "Twisted Tales," Nelson Goodman describes a painting[19] (a "picture biography"
painted by Hato no Chitei in 1069) which demonstrates geographic achrony:

...the organization is geographical rather than chronological, so that scene
x appears to the right of scene y not because incident x occurred before, but
because it occurred east of incident y. (Mitchell 110)

Of course, since a painting does not have a duration in time the way a text can be thought
to—a painting is typically a stasis—what is unusual about this painting is that it has a
sequence of events at all.[20]

---

19   After spending a day reading an argument between Barbara Herrington-Smith and Seymour
Chatman, I found myself in a stranger's apartment. I was looking at her paintings. One of them she described,
to my surprise, as a narrative. The painting in question showed a strange hairless anthropomorphic creature
with somewhat fetal proportions standing on a balcony. Its impossibly long tongue flowed from its mouth over
the railing and a woman was climbing up it. Her description of the painting as narrative struck me as especially
amusing—if Walt Disney's "Cinderella" can be thought of as a contemporary retelling of a pure Ur-Cinderella,
her description implied that the painting was another manifestation of the old "woman climbs the tongue of a
strange hairless anthropomorphic creature with somewhat fetal proportions standing on a balcony" narrative. I
found this less funny after I saw that she had more than one painting that fit this description.
20   Danielle Chynoweth has since pointed out to me that a painting *does* have a duration and sequence:
the order in which the viewer looks at parts of the painting and for how long. This is something the painter is
frequently conscious of and images in painting are discussed in terms of "direction" and where the images lead
the viewer's attention.

> At a certain village in LaMancha, there lived not long ago one of those old-fashioned gentlemen who are never without a lance on a rack, an old shield, a lean horse, and a greyhound

but won't continue. She will finish the cup and turn to the list of Pierre Menard's other works Borges had included, seemingly as a red herring, but where perhaps secret meaning was woven. Here she will find a list of projects, any number of which might be a suitable thesis.

> b) A monograph on the possibility of constructing a poetic vocabulary of concepts that would not be synonyms or paraphrases of those which make up ordinary language, "but ideal objects created by means of common agreement and destined essentially to fill poetic needs" (Nîmes, 1901). (46)

Amy will realize that she no longer has any way to tell if she is sane. Dominique will look up at her and smile.

Amy knows that there is a copy of *Don Quixote* in English underneath the northwest corner of the quad in a time capsule buried in the early 1980s by a group of students staging a performance art funeral of the death of Art and Theory. She does not know that it is being excavated at 8 PM Friday night by a different student for unrelated reasons at the moment the poetry reading at the Jane Addams Bookstore is scheduled to begin as the last ray of sunlight shoots into the hole in the ground and vanishes. Amy and Dominique are approaching the front door and hearing, from the speakers on the street, Becka announce, to the dismay of the management, "Attention customers: all books are one dollar for the next minute..." They are about to laugh and enter.

Sunday	Monday	Tuesday	Wednesday	Thursday	Friday	Saturday
	A1	A1	A1	A1	A1	
A2				Daily Grind	Bowling Alley	A4. Math Library
Chicago	Administ. Building	Dickinson Hall	Stein Hall	Walker Hall	A5. Library, Daily Grind	

DIAGRAM 7

A5: This shows the history A1–5 narrate.

A5 summarizes Amy's efforts to catch up on her thesis. The story explores the idea that an idea can be separated from its original text. Borges' story takes this idea to one of its illogical extremes.

> I've never personally come across this Borges story, but I take it there really is one? If there isn't, hurry up and write it yourself, William! That is, write it as William Gillespie writes a story that Jorge Luis Borges could have written about a guy named Pierre Menard being able to just sit down and spew out Cervantes' *Don Quixote!* You're gonna make so many people absolutely furious! (RT)

B1.

After the poetry reading Becka ran into Amy and Dominique in the Daily Grind. Amy was glazed with enthusiasm and speaking extravagantly about her thesis. She and Becka brainstormed a flood of suggestions until they couldn't stop laughing:

- Amy could write a short story called "Amy, Author of "Jorge Luis Borges, Author of "Pierre Menard, Author of Don Quixote."""" which could be published in a Norton Critical Edition with essays by Northrop Frye and Jean-Paul Sartre;
- then, thus guaranteed admission into the doctoral program of her choice, she could submit a proposal for a dissertation proposing to write Cliffs Notes to the Cliffs Notes for *Don Quixote*, trying to show how entire sentences were lifted intact from the Cliffs Notes to *To Kill a Mockingbird*;
- then, assured tenure, she could write a thousand-page structural analysis of *itself* entitled "Romancing the Comma..."

Dominique said nothing. Amy asked Becka about her thesis. Becka said her thesis was called *I/C*. These two letters stood for Irony and Coincidence, the only things that make the random arbitrary. "In late capitalism, language, once a mirror of reality, suddenly found itself much better than reality. The possibility of a peaceful revolution to overthrow capitalism still existed in language. Reality got up one morning and looked in the mirror and saw something better." That's why she had chosen language as her medium. "Medium" in the sense of being able to contact the spirits. The "thesis" herself would be a book of short "poems." "Poems" as "chance," as "unintentional," as "intuitive," as "inexplicable," and "accidental." She leaned across the table and whispered loudly that she had a computer program capable of generating poetry, but the thought of passing off computer-generated poetry as her own was less exciting to her than the thought of passing off her own poetry as computer-generated. She mentioned LSD, the *I Ching*, and menstrual blood; the conversation ended quickly. Amy was unsure whether she should restrain her laughter. Dominique said nothing but frowned.

2.

Becka was typing in front of a mirror wearing only tights, occasionally pausing to flex. She wore wrist weights and frequently raised one or both arms above her head. She twisted to see the muscles of her back. She touched the curve of her belly. She typed crouching, kneeling, with one hand, with the other, with her pinkies, from an exercycle. She fed herself strawberries, almonds, and chocolate sporadically. She played the Slits and the Breeders and Meredith Monk. She did stretching exercises. She jogged in place. She typed backhand. She paced herself with a stopwatch. She swigged seltzer water and tomato juice from a squeezebottle. She kept notes on a music stand by her chair. She stood on her left foot on her swivel-chair and typed with her right foot. She did curls and presses and lifts. She removed her tights when they were drenched in sweat. She tried to type standing on her head but couldn't manage it. (But how many pushups can Dominique's little body do?)

She wrote.

B1–13. Barthes: *S/Z*

I have referred to two types of models of a story's structure: the prescriptive author's score (my diagrams), and the descriptive narratological model. The original aim of this project was to turn the latter into the former. When a model is used to analyze a story, the process is a metaphoric one. The model becomes the source domain and it is mapped onto the story, the target domain. Like a metaphor, it will reveal some aspects, hide others, and create certain illusions. Freitag's plot triangle, for example, can be mapped onto the film *The Blob*. The process is unlike metaphor in certain ways. In a metaphor, the source domain tends to be more familiar than the target domain — the source domain precedes the target domain. Most of the source domains for the characters' metaphor systems are what Mark Johnson calls "image schemas" — source domains based on generalized categories of physical experience.[21] In the case of the model, the source domain succeeds the target domain: it is a new domain. Examples of models in this sense may include scientific theories and Barthes' transcription of "Sarrasine." The model can then be reapplied to the modeled domain (the cosmos, "Sarrasine") or a different domain (a theory of fluids as a metaphor for women (Irigaray), or the structure of "Sarrasine" as a metaphor for *Don Quixote* (Becka B13)). This reapplication is the process of metaphor. The model becomes a metaphor for the modeled.

Scholes and Martin use *S/Z*'s five codes — a model — as a source domain to understand their respective target domains of James Joyce's "Eveline" and Katherine Mansfield's "Bliss." If another writer were to transcribe or model my story, their model/triangle/transcription would not resemble my scores. This is certain: not only are my scores unconventional, but the story fails to reproduce them in numerous respects I do not care to list. Numerous conflicts arose between my structural intentions and what I wanted to happen in the story, and the latter was, ultimately, privileged. In effect, the story is badly performed.[22]

---

21   I find the term "image schema" somewhat misleading in that most if the image schemas Johnson proposes are more tactile than visual.

22   RS — I would like to see you analyze this "fact" that you note and come to some conclusions about it. What does this suggest theoretically?

3.

She couldn't stop laughing. Consider Roland Barthes' *S/Z*, a book-length study of Honoré de Balzac's "Sarrasine," a short story. The study was much more widely read admired and cited than the story. Becka wasn't sure whether Barthes had ever tried to write a story of his own; but she was pretty sure that no other narratologist would have. From Becka's attempt to rewrite Edgar Allen Poe's "The Gold Bug" as "Sarrasine" it was clear that neither Poe nor Barthes would have recognized the intertext, as somewhere Balzac shifted uncomfortably beneath the bones of two World Wars. Chatman had written that *S/Z* itself deserved a book length study. Becka's plan was to write such a study in such a way that at least two book length studies would be needed to unravel it. Maybe, she thought, Dominique could write them when she was a washed up anagram hag working as a high school librarian.

4.

"Hello?

Why hello Dominique what a surprise.

"Well I know, we haven't spoken in weeks.

"I was writing, Dominique, what were you-

"What a coincidence. This is the last lap, after all.

"That reminds me: I was accepted into Leonora Carrington Arts College.

"Right. Yeah. Near Santa Cruz but more scenic.

"Not a full assistantship, but if I go broke paying tuition I can always live in the woods and forage.

"Seriously. The weather is perfect every day so it's no problem. Lot's of graduate-

"No, silly, a tent.

"Only if it rains so much your books get soaked, but that never-

"Fine. Hey, I saw a copy of Table of Forms.

"Sure, blame me, you're the one who leaves your thesis lying around. That's what you get for writing it.

"Anyway, it's kind of like Lewis Turco on quaaludes.

"I don't know what I meant by that. I'm sorry, I guess that sounded wrong. I thought of a poetic form you forgot to include.

"Really.

"Free verse.

"When?

"No thank you.

"What?

"What?

"Certainly dear, what would you like to ask me?

"In person? It must be important.

"I can take a break from what I'm doing. Can you come over soon?

"See you soon."

LEXIAS	1	2	3	4	5	6	7	8	9	10	11	12	13
Semes	♪		♪	♪			♪	♫			♫		♫
Cultural codes			♪					♪		♪	♪		♫
Antithesis		♩			♩		♩	♩	♩	♩	♩	♩	♩
Enigma 1	𝅝												
"Deep in"		𝅝											
"Hidden"						𝅝							

I never solved the problem of how to perform Barthes' transcription of "Sarrasine." It is a plural problem and invites a multitude of possible solutions. I suspect that, in order to use the five codes to write a new story, one would risk changing Barthes' ideas by articulating them more precisely. S/Z is "a bit maddening in its elliptical, throwaway style." (Chatman, *Story* 115) The fact that B has 13 parts is the only trace of the above transcription that remains from my attempts.

Here is an explanation of the five codes with some consideration given to their use as tools to write. Barthes lists them "without trying to put them in any order of importance." (19) I, however, do. I have listed them in order of usefulness from least to most.

SYM Symbolic Code (Voice of Symbol)—Barthes discusses the symbolic logic of "Sarrasine" in terms of antitheses. Because the antitheses in the opening of "Sarrasine" are so pronounced, the code would appear to be formulated to explain them. It is unclear how to use this code to interpret other stories or write new ones. Wallace Martin finds examples of antitheses in Katherine Manfield's "Bliss" (164) and Robert Scholes finds examples in James Joyce's "Eveline." (102-3) In B7 I use symmetry as an alternative symbolic logic.

REF Reference Code (Code of Science) — "They constitute the text's references to things already 'known' and codified by a culture." (Scholes 100) These "things" can be "physical, physiological, medical, psychological, literary, historical, etc." (*S/Z* 20)

5.

Becka suspected she knew what it was. She lit incense. She took down a hand-drawn chart from the bulletin board above her computer and tacked up some Rorschach blots. She poured a can of dice onto her desktop. She set up a Ouija board pointing to Q. She played a recording of the Tibetan Monks. She did ginseng. She tried to figure out the lotus position. She pulled the shrinkwrap from a pack of tarot cards and, not sure how to use them, dealt a game of solitaire. She tried to warm up her lava lamp but the knock came too quickly. Becka opened the door and when she moved left, Dominique moved right. They mirrored each other. But they didn't look alike. Though they were both short. But they didn't notice that. Their bodies were different. They were familiar with each others' bodies. They looked. Becka had been working out. Dominique noticed this but had no words for it; she merely noted that Becka seemed somehow stronger. They looked. They made weak jokes about how they hadn't seen each other in awhile.

6.

"What did you want to talk to me about?"

7.

Dear Becka,

There is no longer you and I, only a broken mirror in which when I go to my left, you go to your left. Does this mean it is you *or* I? In order for the mirror to work properly, we would have to stand very still and stare at each other, each concentrating and subtly contorting towards symmetry. Once in this position, there would be the comfort of no longer wondering which of us was the other's reflection, each of us immobile. But whoever made the first move towards her notebook would shatter the other. How can we work together on something if our every motion is mutually contradictory?

You like me, you like me not, I like you, I like you not, you like me... there is a field of rosepetals in a pattern repeating into infinity. It is the universe my thoughts roam, proposing and rejecting various constellations. It is silent. And the untalked-about gets thought about, rings of useless language form, thicken, twist into intricate braids and mobius strips, clouds, planetary systems, and obscure the light in systems too complex to decay slowly, supernova, the metaphor consumes itself in a warm blaze of wasted energy.

This is why I can't talk to you about it. Then, in addition to the suspicion that all suspicions were false including that one, and the agonizing symmetrical asymmetry, there would be the danger of recursion. We would be talking together about talking together. Then no conclusion would ever be reached because, viciously, recursion is not nuanced. Nobody can appreciate the subtle difference between three levels of recursion and four: two is infinite. So here we are: narcissistic in each others' solipsism. And the signifier refers to itself until the metaphor expands to exclude the universe.

It is difficult to understand what this excludes. As Barthes admits, "all codes are cultural." (*S/Z* 18) I cannot say what details of my story are not cultural. However, the story takes place within a very small subculture: the world of graduate studies in English. My story is, in this sense, inaccessible. Nine workshop participants confessed to not being interested in theory (all of them (except the instructor) graduate students in English) and the tenth was irate at how poorly theory was represented. Each mention of a theoretical term, idea, or writer calls for specialized knowledge on the part of the reader.

SEM Semes (Voice of Person)—This is the code in which Barthes explores the idea of the character. He describes characters as a series of semes accumulated by a "Proper Name," or even a pronoun (Barthes *S/Z* 191). I have already discussed the strategies of characterization I am using. I would consider each manifestation of the characters' metaphor systems to be a seme, though there may be other semes as well.

ACT Code of Actions (Voice of Empirics)—The movements and actions of the characters. These tend to come in namable clusters. For easily understood reasons, they often occur in pairs. When the door knocks, Becka opens it. When Becka kisses Dominique, Dominique pulls away. These tiny set-ups and follow-throughs, no matter how banal, give a story a certain momentum.

HER Hermeneutic Code (Voice of Truth)—This code pairs questions with answers, and so suggests double units. Barthes refines this opening and closing into a list of ten possible stages. This code is not reversible.

> In certain kinds of stories, such as detective stories, the hermeneutic code dominates the entire discourse. Together with the code of actions it is responsible for narrative suspense, for the readers' desire to complete, to finish the text. (Scholes, 100)

I will never give you this letter. Love, Dominique

8.

Dominique's eyes scanned Becka's bookshelf from across the room. "A couple of things. I need your help. I want to overthrow the seminar. I have a plan to drive the dominant students into silence."

"What kind of plan?"

"Goes like this. Whenever a student interrupts another, you will cough. Whenever anybody says something irrelevant to establish their own credibility, I will jingle my keys. Whenever somebody insults the text, Amy will pop her gum. Whenever anybody says "postmodern…""

"Why?"

"The fact that there are people who don't talk is the fault of the people who do. Amy can't-"

"What's the point in overthrowing 255C Dickinson Hall? Rising up against Marxists?"

"Gotta start somewhere."

"Get in the game."

"I don't need that kind of exercise. I want a new game. Are you worried about your grade?"

"No. Chrzastowski loves me. "

9.

Becka watched Dominique's eyes play across the dice: tetrahedrons, octahedrons, dodecahedrons, icosahedrons, and, she realized with satisfaction, imperfect solids whose shapes Dominique couldn't name. Becka looked through Dominique's coffee-colored skin and her black avalanche of curls.

Becka was ready to win a fight with Dominique. When Dominique put her hands on her hips, Becka crossed her arms. When Dominique raised her voice, Becka stood on a chair. When Dominique refused to look at her, Becka turned off the lights and crashed a cymbal. When Dominique said nothing, Becka put on loud music. When Dominique turned it off, Becka sang it. Dominique whistled around Becka's teardrop. Dominique spilled broke and bled. Becka, through fermenting, turned into a diamond. She would saw her way out of this cocoon and flutter away, leaving Dominique to depressurize.

Of these five codes, the hermeneutic code strikes me as the most useful and revealing. It is one of the consistencies carried over from Barthes' 1966 essay "Introduction to the Structural Analysis of the Narrative," in which he called them "Nuclei" or "cardinal functions."[23] Using structural narratology's guiding metaphor—the story is a sentence— Barthes lists the ten possible parts of the Hermeneutic sentence:

1	thematization
2	proposal
3	formulation of the enigma
4	promise of an answer (or request for an answer)
5	snare
6	equivocation
7	jamming
8	suspended answer
9	partial answer
10	disclosure (210)

In B3–13 I attempted to play through the hermeneutic sentence one stage at a time. The enigma is: what does Dominique need to talk to Becka about? In B5 I attempted the impossible: I tried to reverse the hermeneutic code and move from answer to question. I begin with a false answer—they looked alike—and tried to transform it into a question: what did they look like?

10.	They mirrored each other.
9.	But they didn't look alike.
8.	Though they were both short.
7.	But they didn't notice that.
6.	Their bodies were different.
5.	They were familiar with each others' bodies.
4.	They looked at each others' bodies.
3.	Becka had been working out.
2.	Dominique noticed this but had no words for it.
1	They looked.

---

23   Chatman and Martin have each discussed the evolution of Barthes' ideas between 1966 and 1970. Barthes' "Introduction to the Structural Analysis of the Narrative" is admittedly a more appropriate object of my study than *S/Z*, in that the earlier essay makes claims to universality. But who can resist *S/Z*?

10.

Dominique put down the poem Becka had just finished. "The worst thing about your thesis is that it's an interesting idea. The idea may be more interesting than the writing."

"That doesn't make sense. The idea *is* the writing."

"In this case, I'm not sure. The idea is suitably whimsical but I don't know if it's applicable."

"Barthes never claimed his ideas were applicable. "

"Why hide the structure?"

"Why flesh out a skeleton? Why give a chassis a car? Why ruin a motor by putting it in something?"

"Poetry is a machine covered in wrapping paper?"

"Poetry is a performance with rules."

"Unless you explain the rules, you are making an Eskimo watch a basketball game. What rules?"

"You score, then you find out."

"I'm not sure I know what you mean by score. This is reductive. In addition to not giving Barthes credit, you do a disservice to his ideas."

"It's a plural text. If I have to modify, change, adapt Barthes' ideas in order to articulate them, I have to admit I get a kind of sexy thrill from sneaking into an arena of discourse I'm not qualified for. I am liberating ideas from theory, which is incapable of helping those who most need it."

"That's like liberating the product from the workers. We consume ketchup and attribute it to Heinz. We consume french fries and agree that they are saltier than McDonald's earlier works. There is labor behind your thesis: yours and other people's. You need to show who wrote it and how."

"You think that's social, but it isn't. The ketchup, the sign, the text, mean differently to everyone. To insist upon a single explanation of them is not social at all. The same moon is seen by everybody but..."

"The moon was not built, let's at least not confuse nature and artifact..."

"...and insist upon confusing author and employee? What kind of explanation do you want on ketchup bottles? I'm sure you could find one boasting that the recipe was the ingenuity of a man named Heinz, omitting the fact that he plagiarized his wife Maric,

I find an interesting demonstration in the second chapter of Thomas Pynchon's *The Crying of Lot 49*. The chapter is a narrative juggling act: Pynchon trying to suspend as many questions and half-completed actions in the air as he can. He takes five pairs of shoes and drops one of each of them. In this chapter, there is so much happening simultaneously that only the banality (expectedness (Barthes, *S/Z* 139)) of what is happening makes the scene intelligible, and only the simultaneity makes it interesting. In general, Pynchon's enigmas do not resolve: he writes hermeneutic sentence fragments. This is one of the aspects of his fiction which, at first, seems innovative: he writes gargantuan novels with no payoff.[24]

One of the things I like the most about *S/Z* is the chapter devoted to it in Rosalind Coward and John Ellis' *Language and Materialism*:

> To understand *S/Z* as anything other than a superior formal method.... We must first understand the relation between realism and the plurality of language.

> First, realism stresses the product and not the production. It represses production in the same way that the mechanism of the market, of general exchangeability, represses production in a capitalist society. It does not matter where a product comes from, how it was made, by whom or for what purpose it was intended.... In the same way, it does not matter that realism is produced by a certain use of language, by a complex production; all that matters is the illusion, the story, the content.... We do not look at the production, but the product; hence the shock of reading an unusual book like *S/Z*, which goes against the 'natural' way of reading realist texts, and looks precisely at the way the illusion is produced....

> Language is treated as though it stands in for, is identical with, the real world. The business of realist writing is, according to its philosophy, to be the equivalent of a reality, to imitate it. This 'imitation' is the basis of realist literature, and its technical name is *mimesis*, mimicry.... (46–7)

---

24   RS—Again, I would like to see you work out the theoretical significance of this. The weakness of your "eclectic" approach is that you have a tendency to abandon your insights, questions, and problems, rather than developing, nurturing, tarrying with them. WG—The weakness of your grading is a tendency to find fault with the lack of tedium and to focus on what is not present, rather than to notice this wet, massive slab of love throbbing in your lap that your dry-as-dust, wheezing, juiceless theory improbably spawned. Is eighty pages of passionate engagement not enough for you?

making no mention that the ingenuity was in the inexpensive means of production, and not natural talent with corn syrup. The credit my thesis owes is not to Barthes, who was doing what he wanted, but to the treecutters, the programmers, the typesetters, proofreaders, editors—the one who called up Barthes and asked him if "unreaderly" was a typo—translators..."

"I'm starving. Mind if I smoke?"

"Suit yourself."

"Gotta light?"

"Yeah. Here."

"Thanks. I have no argument that what Barthes did counts as "hard work" to anyone who has ever experienced hard work. But how do you make readers into writers? How do you teach new languages by speaking in them? I don't know. This is like Queneau and Perec clashing horns on a mountaintop..."

"You've got the hair for it. Have another cigarette."

11.

Becka grabbed Dominique and kissed her. (You love me.) With her teeth she imprinted Dominique's lip. (You are being monogamous with Amy purely as an excuse to stop having sex with me.) Becka traced the perimeter of Dominique's ear with her fingers, remembering numbers, trying every combination she could. (Amy's writing is nothing like ours.) With her fingernails in the small of Dominique's back, Becka scrawled hasty pacts. (You helped me when I thought I was a girl, just like you are helping Amy now.) Becka touched Dominique's lip with her tongue. (When I was trying to master cursive, you had piano lessons, horseback riding lessons, and piano lessons—your talent is expensive, not natural.)

When Dominique pulled away Becka pushed her away.

Becka said: "you're beautiful when you hate me."

Dominique said nothing.

Realism is aesthetically and politically questionable, no doubt. By claiming to represent reality, a story is defining reality. This alone does not trouble me. It is more a question of whether I want to live in the reality it offers.[25] In *S/Z*, it is arguable whether Barthes is showing the production of "Sarrasine." It seems unlikely that what Barthes derives from the story is what Balzac had in mind. Nevertheless, Barthes manages to show an apparatus at work whose function is to establish, thwart, and fulfill a readers' expectations while remaining invisible.[26]

I will call the metaphor Coward and Ellis propose stories are products. The product is the source domain and the story is the target domain. Companies are mapped onto writers, buyers are mapped onto readers, and the machinery of production is mapped onto the conventions of realist fiction. This metaphor reveals that books are indeed produced and sold and that the reader may be unaware of the details of the production. It conceals the fact that an author is not, in the strictest sense, a company. Though an author may work for money, may respond to the pressures of the marketplace, and may even have editors who act as bosses, her value may reside more in her individuality than in her efficiency. The metaphor creates the illusion that an author will only conceal her decision-making to prevent the reader from finding out about it. Sometimes an author may conceal her decision making to allow the reader the pleasure of figuring it out for themselves.[27]

---

25   RS—Is it therefore impossible to "represent reality"?
26   RS—Is narrative solely produced in an author's mind? Where does he get his materials? What kind of labor does he rely on?
27   RS—To return to Jason's question in class, one wonders where the unconscious appears in this scheme of things.

12.

"Well, Dominique, what do you have to say for yourself?"

"I don't want to kiss you tonight Becka."

"Apparently not."

"I came here to ask if you had marijuana."

"What do you mean?"

"To sell."

"No."

"Sure you do."

"No. What do I look like? I've always shared with you. Suddenly you'd rather buy it, keep me at arm's length, smoke up with Amy."

"Can you get me high?"

13.

"No."

After Dominique left Becka ignited a rocket and, with the exhaust vapors playing about her nostrils, began typing. She stayed up until 8AM and SarrasiniZed *Don Quixote*, consulting three library copies she had checked out, she chuckled, to be thorough. She kept them in her closet, she cackled, to be safe.

[1]Don Quixote

[2]I was deep in a certain village in LaMancha [3]where dwell even the most old-fashioned of men, in the midst of nothing to do. [4]The break of day occurred outside the inn. [5]Seated on a horse [6]and hidden behind the sinuous folds of a suit of armor [7]I could contemplate at my leisure the windmills across the plain I was riding across. [8]The windmills, partially covered with snow, stood out dimly against the grayish background of a cloudy sky, barely whitened by the moon. Seen amid these fantastic surroundings, they vaguely resembled giants half out of their shrouds, a gigantic representation of the famous books of chivalry...

C1.

I know you won't accept my statement in this form.

But the story is the basic unit of human experience. Emotions happen.

I care for my students in a way I can't articulate. Love doesn't translate well into English. It looks bad in a teaching portfolio. Show me a pedagogy in this institution that necessitates love. They don't love me. They admire me, but most of my virtuosity is in what I hide from them. For example, I have hidden from them my belief that theory is politically ineffectual. In that it came with a salary, it has, in fact, ruined me. I no longer notice the labor in anything.

I bought new lawn furniture last weekend.

I must hide this from them.

I am more interested in imagining their lives than I am in living my own.

Dominique, for example. This morning a colleague of mine who teaches creative writing was complaining about Dominique. I asked Dominique about it. Dominique said she had written a story with 26 paragraphs, each of which was six lines long and began with each subsequent letter of the alphabet. In the first paragraph, which began with A, every word had the letter A. In the second paragraph, which began with B, every word had either an A or a B. And so on. By paragraph 5, the constraint posed little challenge. So she added the constraint that, throughout the entire story, every two adjacent words had at least one letter in common. This second constraint was designed to take over as the first constraint loosened. Since every word in the first paragraph had the letter A in common, the second constraint was at first inoperable but tightened slowly. She mentioned Howard Bergerson (I think) and Walter Abish (whoever they are). She had told her class none of this, and they didn't notice. She was afraid that if she told them, they would lose interest, relegate the work to an irrelevant, unnamed category of literature different from true fiction, and consider her a proofreader rather than an author. My colleague simply thought she had written a bad story to annoy him.

I wonder what she would think of this. I wonder how wrong I am.

Once in my seminar I saw her finish a word square starting with Cixous. She must have been painfully bored. I wanted to ask if I could copy it down, but I thought she might be embarrassed to be caught doodling. This is all I remember:

C1. Cohn: Narrated Monologue

In C1–8 I attempted to make sense out of point of view. My results (to quote Scholes referring to Genette) "may not have sufficient analytic value to justify their taxonomic complexity." (97) Ultimately, every distinction I explored (from the rudimentary distinction of show vs. tell to the more complex distinctions of omniscient, limited omniscient, fly-on-the-wall, camera's eye, and Genette's model based on verb forms) collapsed under my probing. Even my attempts to demonstrate what each model reveals, conceals, and creates the illusion of, have proven too convoluted to narrate. I will indicate these complications only by pointing out two conventions of narrative that seem to defy grammar itself.

Martin points to the first sentence of Ernest Hemingway's "The Short Happy Life of Francis Macomber": "It was now lunchtime and they were all sitting under the double green fly of the tent pretending that nothing had happened." (Martin 136-7) "It was now" would appear to be a grammatical impossibility. Martin implies that this construction is only a function of the third person narration but I disagree. "Having read his chapter on point of view, I was now very confused" is an example of the same thing. Another conventional impossibility of narrative is identified by Dorit Cohn: the narrated monologue. Cohn identifies three ways a character's thoughts can be represented:

Quoted Monologue	*Narrated Monologue*	*Psycho-Narration*
(He thought:) I am late.	He was late.	He knew he would be late. (6-7)

These examples are insufficient: only the context could distinguish "He was late" as a narrated monologue rather than straight narration. "Cloaked in the grammar of narration, a sentence rendering a character's opinion can look every bit like a sentence relating a fictional fact." (6) The narrated monologue represents, in the third person, the exact thoughts of a character who is narrated in the third person.[28] It is neither a quotation of their thoughts (quoted monologue) nor a reporting of them (psycho-narration). It replaces the grammatical inconsistency of the quoted monologue (which leaps from third to first person) with a stylistic inconsistency, or a shift in "voice." Consider the overwritten one-

28   In the workshop we were discussing (another student's) story written in the second person. Many students found the device ineffective because we could not identify with the character we were being addressed as. One of the students protested these complaints by explaining that she read it as a narrated monologue: as if the character were thinking in the second person. (KD) This suggests that the narrated monologue is not limited to the third person, though it is hard to imagine how it could be in the first person.

```
C  I  X  O  U  S
I     A     N     T
X  A  N  A  D  U
O     A     U     D
U  N  D  U  L  Y
S  T  U  D  Y  S
```

sentence paragraphs in A2: they are Amy's thoughts, in her mental "voice," related in the third person.

C2.

Tonight in the seminar she said nothing. She was apparently writing a transcript of the class:

Mr. C: I'd like to start us off today by problematizing all the assigned reading. Does it make sense to speak universally of a narrative situation?

Becka: Can't we instead say that a real author wrote the story because she got off on it?

Eric: [Crosses his arms. Asserts that he's not sure about that. Brings up a book nobody else has read.]

George: [Has also read that book.]

Becka: *S/Z* elides many of these questions by speaking of the plural text, which implies an infinity of narrators and narratees.

Amy: What about the reader?

Iain: [Corrects her: "narratee"]

Becka: Not everyone believes in the reader.

John: [Says that reading *S/Z* is like wrestling with mist.]

George: [Apologizes on behalf of the entire class]

Fabio: [Interrupts, removes glasses, touches beard, says something agonizingly ponderous with frequent groping pauses midsentence, leaving no space between sentences]

Iain: [Tells Fabio he didn't understand that at all]

Fabio: [Shrugs, grins, begins an expansive handgesture, opens mouth]

Mr. C: [Cuts Fabio off] I think we should return to an interesting question Becka brought up. One thing we might think about is, oddly enough, grammar. Person and verb tense already situate the narrator with respect to the narration. Even if the story is clearly fictional, an implied person is speaking from an implied point in time, usually past tense: after the narrative is over. What else might we think about?

Becka: Dominique, would you like to share some of the things you're scribbling down over there?

Dominique: No.

George: [Mentions another text]

Iain: [Indicates that *that* author couldn't write her way out of a wet paper bag]

[laughter]

C2. Chatman: Voice

While Cohn's "Narrated Monologue" is elusive, Chatman's "Voice" is downright slippery:

REAL AUTHOR ⇒

IMPLIED AUTHOR ⇒ NARRATOR ⇒ NARRATEE ⇒ IMPLIED READER ⇒

REAL READER ("Voice" 9)

Rimmon-Kenan has proven helpful in articulating Chatman's idea more clearly. First of all, neither of them consider the real author and real reader to be relevant to the narrative. According to Rimmon-Kenan's corrected version of this model, the implied author and reader are voiceless, silent constructs. The narrator and narratee are essential, rather than optional as Chatman proposes. Distinctions between the implied author and narrator; and between the implied reader and narratee, are very difficult to identify.[29] Chatman

---

29   There are unconventional stories where an implied author is identifiable. Raymond Queneau wrote a pornographic novel using a an assumed Irish pseudonym and identity. In Augusto Monterroso's "Leopoldo: His Labors." the implied reader and author are separable from the narrator and narratee because of the device of inserting a text within a text:

> After some time, he felt relatively confident. He prepared a good amount of paper, demanded quiet throughout the house, put on a green eyeshade to protect his eyes from the harmful effects of the electric light, cleaned his pen, made himself as comfortable as possible in his chair, chewed his nails, looked intelligently at a patch of clear sky, and slowly, interrupted only by the beating of his impassioned heart, he wrote:

> "....When he reached the country with his best friend who was the little dog being that he was a widower the flowers were very pretty it was spring and in that season the flowers are very pretty being that it is their season."

> Leopoldo was not lacking in critical sense. He knew his style was not very good. The next day he bought a rhetoric and a grammar. Both confused him even more. Both taught how to write well but not how to avoid writing badly.

> The following year, however, with fewer preparations, he was ready to write:

> "....In this sweet season there are brightly colored flowers in abundance, with dazzling corollas to delight the eye of the dusty pilgrim, and the mellifluous chirp of the happy and trusting little birds is a feast for the delicate ear of the thirsty traveler. Oh Fabius, how beautiful is the countryside in spring!"

> He had learned his rhetoric and his grammar well. (55-6)

In this story, the contrast between the competent style of the narrator contrasted with his admiration of Leopoldo's writing inexplicably separates the two. The humor relies on this. The implied author and reader, who together share the knowledge that the narrator is pompous and has mistaken Leopoldo for a genius, share a laugh over the head of the narrator and the narratee.

C3.

I sat in my office for twenty minutes staring at the blinking light on my voice mail before I picked up the phone and pressed the button.

I got a strange feeling in my throat.

I stared at the Chatman text on my office shelf.

I remembered the way Dominique had been silent. I remembered how naive yet talkative Amy had been, unaware that her car was being towed outside. I wondered what Becka was thinking. Why did she say that sex is random, gender arbitrary? Was she aware that her thinking was an academicized manifestation of the American "whatever" disease, that her attitude always made me lose interest in her writing before I even looked at it? Anyone who didn't continuously look for order was mystical and full of shit.

"Professor Chrzastowski? This is Dominique. I wanted to talk to you about the seminar. I know its late but I thought I'd ask if you wanted to go have a beer. Call 344 6583 if you get this message. Bye."

"Steve, this is Debbie. Can you pick up some asparagus on the way home tonight? I'm making vegan loaf for my Zen group tomorrow. Thanks hon."

I remembered the way Dominique had been silent.

I picked up the phone.

suggests that an implied author can sometimes be detected by comparing different works by the same real author. He also suggests that in the case of the unreliable narrator, the distinction is prominent because the unreliable narrator's "values diverge strikingly from that of the implied author" (9).

In C1, professor Chrzastowski is revealed to be the narrator. The narratee is implied, but not revealed, through the use of the second person. The narrator and narratee would seem to both be well-read. It is difficult for me to characterize the implied author of my story: "…implied authors are often far superior in intelligence and moral standards to the … real authors." (Rimmon-Kenan 86-87)[30]

---

30   RS—Perhaps s/he is your textual unconscious; perhaps s/he must be read by an Other—an analyst of whatever kind.

C4.

red neon	cigarette smoke	Janis Joplin	spearmint gum	nervous tension	A.B.TOKLAS'
door					
smoke					ENTRANCE
pool table		conversation		smooth wood	
crowd					"Excuse me."
her					"Hello."
smile of	alcohol	billiards break			"Hi."
recognition					
stool				wobbly stool	"What can I get
bartender			spearmint gum		you?"
curls		laughter			
eyes					SAINT PAULI
nose					GIRL
smile				her elbow	
chin	sandalwood oil	pinball			"Same as she's
necklace					having."
hands					
money					"Three dollars."
coaster		laughter		cold glass	
mug					VIRGINIA
fingers					WIDES 120
silver ring			beer		
cigarette	beer	cashregister			"I didn't know
lips				her elbow	you smoked."
eyelashes					
match					"I don't."
squint		Joni Mitchell	beer		
fingers					"Me neither."
purse				somebody else's	
smile				elbow	"Want one?"
smoke	cigarette smoke	coins in jar			
teeth			beer		"Yeah, actually."
eyes					
fingers				gum under bar	"Perfect."
copper ring		low rough voice			
fingernails					"Thank you."
cigarette				cigarette	
match	matchsmoke		beer	cigarette	"Why did you
flame	cigarette	glass breaking	cigarette		choose to meet
eyes	cigarette		cigarette	dizziness	me here? Not
smile	cigarette		cigarette		because its close
cigarette	cigarette		cigarette	choking	to Austen State."
smoke	cigarette	pinball tilt	cigarette		
smoke	cigarette		cigarette	burning	"Exactly."
smoke	cigarette		cigarette		
ashtray	cigarette		cigarette	calm	
arm	cigarette	laughter	beer		
bracelet	cigarette				

C3. Mazza: Point of View

In trying to hammer out a theory of point of view I began with grammar: first, second, and third person; and verb tense. In C1 (in the essay), I demonstrated that narration has conventions which seem to thwart ordinary grammar. Abandoning, for the time being, consideration of grammar, I went on to consider point of view as access by a narrator (who could be a character) to historical information (events in the story) and thoughts (of other characters and even their own). Uneasily, I proposed four types of narrator:

1. An external observer who narrates actions and dialogue. (camera, fly-on-the-wall)
2. An internal observer capable of narrating the characters' conscious thoughts.
3. An external omniscient narrator who knows things about the history the characters do not.
4. An internal omniscient narrator capable who knows the characters' unconscious motivations

This gives us the external observer, internal observer, external omniscient, and internal omniscient narrators. It is possible for a narrator to be any combination of these. It is possible for a first person narrator to be an observer of themselves but not omniscient—I do not see how a character can know more than they know. An internal omniscient narrator may be connected to a single person (*The Catcher in the Rye*) or to many (*To the Lighthouse*), and even, conceivably, more than one character at a time.

Cris Mazza's story "Is It Sexual Harassment Yet?" is a story written in two columns—two simultaneous points of view. These two points of view concern two different characters but differ in many other respects as well. The question this raises— what necessitates two columns?—has resulted in C3-8. In my story, everything on the same line happens at the same time. Mazza's story is not like that: the two columns do not seem to synch up in time. In fact, the two points of view she establishes are so different that her two characters do not always seem to be in the same story. Furthermore, "the title raises a question" which is never satisfactorily answered (Barthes *S/Z* 17). I have adapted and changed Mazza's technique in various ways to explore distinctions of point of view. C3 takes place in Professor Chrzastowski's office immediately after his seminar. It is late at night. The central column narrates his interior monologue: internal observer. The left and right columns are external observers: a camera's eye and a microphone's ear respectively.

C5.

(How did we get on this topic?)

"I'm not monogamous so much as married."

(Finally.)

"Why?" (You know better than that.)

(Acquiescence)

"I- We want to have children, my wife and I"

"Why?" (Oh, *that...*)

(You're not supposed to ask that.)

"These are very hard questions."

"Yes." (You should know the answers by now.)

(Whew. What an amazing person.)

"Are you nonmonogamous?"

"Not at the moment. I think I need a new word. Nonmonogamy defines the practice negatively. The name implies a lack of constraints. I think it should only be practiced as constraints. Rules, like never sleeping with the same person twice in a row, or the same sex of person. Prescriptive, definitely, not as a way to retroactively inscribe order on a social life. When people are nonmonogamous but simply don't tell their lovers about each other, I don't consider that nonmonogamy. The paradigm of monogamy will structure any relationship unless it is explicitly challenged. Like it has with Amy and I." (No.)

(I'm not supposed to ask that.)

(constraints?)

(you mean be exclusively not sexually exclusive?)

(Wow. Oh. Uh,)

"I wanted so badly to experiment too, back at Antioch, but I had to make absolutely sure not to be a rapist."

(Oops, I mean...)

"Was that difficult?" (What?)

C4. Thornton: Showing

From our own strictly analytic point of view it must be added (as Booth's discussion, moreover, reveals in passing) that the very idea of showing, like that of imitation or narrative representation (and even more so, because of its naively visual character), is completely illusory: in contrast to dramatic representation, no narrative can "show" or "imitate" the story it tells. All it can do is tell it in a manner which is detailed, precise, "alive," and in that way give more or less the illusion of mimesis—which is the only narrative mimesis, for this single and sufficient reason: that narration, oral or written, is a fact of language, and language signifies without imitating. (Genette, *Story and Discourse* 164)

For Robbe-Grillet, the function of language is not a raid on the absolute, a violation of the abyss, but a progression of names over a surface, a patient unfolding that will gradually "paint" the object, caress it, and along its whole extent deposit a patina of tentative identification, no single term of which could stand by itself for the presented object. (Barthes, "Objective Literature" 12)

The gaze is the basic unit of human experience.
(and if you're blind?)
Morning birdsong is the basic unit of human experience.
(and if you're deaf?)
The tongue touching the roof of one's mouth is the basic unit of human experience. Odor of unwashed armpit; or cut grass. And so it goes. I want to smell something in this jazz, even if its cigar smoke. I think when you reached page [22], you knew this too... (RT)

The crucial distinction, therefore, is not between telling and showing, but between different degrees and kinds of telling. (Rimmon-Kenan 108)

(Go:)

"The rapist, as he is misconstrued in this culture, is not your uncle. He emerges from shadows. He is anonymous. The myth is a denial that rape is intrinsic to our culture and family structure and that rapists can be friendly, popular, public people. In my friendships, I tried to be emotionally present, gentle, and tentative about sex. So I slept with and cared for many women, but didn't have sex."

(Yikes! My uncle, but how could he.. he couldn't possibly... he's speaking figuratively.)

(Relaxrelaxrelax...)

(It's wonderful to hear this.)

"What about men?" (Phobe.)

(Thank you.)

"Never cared much for them."

"Why not?" (Me neither.)

(Cut it out.)

"It still happens to me too. Even though I'm married and, in some states, it is legal for me to rape my wife; I'm still afraid. Sometimes during sex I'll feel as though I'm raping Debbie and freeze up or start to cry and want to just hold her. I'm sure she finds this quite frustrating, but she's understanding about it. I'm pretty sure I caught her masturbating this morning. In the shower."

(What?)

(It's weird to hear this.)

"*Caught* her?" (Poor woman.)

(Why *does* she hide?)
(Am I drunk?)

"Found her, I mean, she caught herself. I don't mind. Tell me something."

"Class was great. You're a sensitive lecturer." (I'm attracted to you.)
(Where did that come from?)

"Thanks."

"I'm attracted to you."

(What?)

C5. Lakoff: Narrative and Society

To follow a standard narrative of the academic paper, it would have been appropriate to begin by proclaiming the death of narrative, or by announcing that there is a crisis in twentieth century literature, or by affixing the prefix "post-" to a word it hasn't been affixed to yet. Instead I began by confessing that I couldn't decide what narrative was, or, more specifically, what wasn't a narrative. It would have been easier and flashier simply to announce the failure of narratology and gloat. I make no specific claims as to the importance of this project. Narrative, however, is important. Narratives, like metaphors, bring a prefabricated cultural understanding to many complicated situations, reveal and conceal aspects of life, and create certain illusions. Given that familiar narratives are often used as tools of understanding, what they reveal is seldom unique. What they conceal is sometimes murder.

In his essay "Metaphor and War: The Metaphor System used to Justify War in the Persian Gulf," George Lakoff explores the metaphor system used by the Bush administration in 1990 and 1991 when it made its intentions about Iraq-occupied Kuwait clear. The "target" domain being the situation in the Middle East, the source domain selected by the administration was a narrative—a narrative Lakoff describes as "The Fairytale of the Just War." In this narrative, there is a victim, a villain, and a hero. Lakoff shows that, in the administration's first attempt to explain their intentions in the Persian Gulf, this metaphor was mapped with the United States citizens as the victim, the U.S. military as the hero, and, of course, Saddam Hussein as a metonym for Iraq, the villain. After a nationwide poll revealed that this mapping was not going to generate enough public support in that it amounted to trading lives for oil, the administration provided a second mapping of the metaphor, this time with Kuwait as victim. I will not dwell on the various ways in which Kuwait—an extremely wealthy nation—can be shown to have victimized Iraq and other Arab nations. In the beginning of his "Address to the Nation on the Commencement of the Bombing of Iraq" speech, Bush describes Kuwait as a "small and helpless neighbor." As the events of the war show clearly, Kuwait was in no way helpless. Bush was stamping a neat triangle from an overwhelming, complicated, and highly suspect blob of international economic relations.

To paraphrase Lakoff, narratives can kill. I do not demonstrate this in the story.

C6.

They walked through cobblestone streets.

He asked to see her bracelet. She offered him her hand.

He looked at her bracelet, which had a key hanging from a beaded cord.

He kept her hand. It curled around his.

They walked down cobblestone streets beneath dim streetlamps.

They passed a house where a book Dominique had been searching for for years—*Gadsby* by Ernest Vincent Wright, was taped up in a box in the basement.

They passed Becka's house, where Amy and Becka were engaged in an impromptu performance of *Wuthering Heights* using sock puppets. They did not see them.

They passed a bush with a twenty dollar bill in it and another with a person sleeping in it.

He couldn't get this P.J Harvey song out of his head.

He imagined other faculty members peering from the windows of the dark houses they passed.

That morning, he had misplaced his housekey and couldn't open the deadbolt to leave. Debbie was in the shower with, for some reason, the door locked, and he had to knock so she would open the door so he could ask if she had seen his keys which she hadn't and he imagined being trapped at home forever for a moment and then remembered where he put them and apologized and left.

He had heard it that morning on his clock radio as it woke him from a dream about Dominique, none of which he remembered.

He also couldn't remember that before he started having nightmares at age 5 when he tried to get into his locked parents' bedroom in the middle of the night because he thought they were being eaten by monsters.

He never knew they were having sex.

Instead, on a smaller interpersonal scale, I show how socially understood narratives structure the lives of the characters.[31] For example, when Dominique and the professor express physical affection for one another, this leads to a clumsy sexual encounter because of certain social narratives. The narrative of heterosexual relations reveals their love for one another, creates the illusion that they should have sex, and conceals a world of possible ways of structuring their friendship. When Amy finds out, she flies into a rage. The narrative of monogamy and jealousy reveals that she was genuinely disturbed by the events, creates the illusion that Dominique has betrayed her and their romance must end, and conceals a world of possible reactions as well as the fact that Dominique's feelings for Amy never changed. Dominique, locked out of her own apartment by the jealous Amy, is caught in the pull of these narratives and begins to confess guilt and resentment of her professor that she doesn't actually feel. The professor, also caught in the pull of these narratives, expects that his wife will be furious at him and, when she is not, is paradoxically forced to question her affection for him in the first place. In A2-4, it was my intention to show that Amy and Dominique's love for each other, not being heterosexual, falls outside of most conventional social romantic narratives. It would be difficult for them to get married and have kids and live happily ever after, and their romance will not be universally encouraged by society in the ways many heterosexual romances seem to be. The ecstasy they feel that causes them to stay in the bathtub for days and have sex on a train is the ecstasy of a love which society has not constructed: a romance relevant to them.

I object to war. I do not object to narrative. I want narratives to be used as tools of understanding consciously and deliberately. I want social narratives to be identified, problematized, and replaced.[32]

---

31   RS—I'm losing coherence here; can you further articulate the difference between "narratives that kill" and narratives that "structure the lives of characters"? WG—In the following sentences I explain how narratives strucutre the lives of characters. Narratives that kill: "Liberate the people of Iraq." "War on terror." "You're either with us or you're against us." "Bringing peace to Southeast Asia." "Making the world safe for democracy." "Let's roll." "Shock and awe." "Operation Enduring Freedom." "Operation Infinite Justice."

32   RS—But how does one guarantee that narratives lead to understanding and not to obfuscation as in your Gulf War example above? WG—This is an excellent question and, indeed, I wish we spent time in seminar working out an answer to it.

C7.

If I could take that key, unlock your belly button, open your legs, walk into the cosmos, and read all your writing, I would.

The alcohol has slowed the exhilaration of being near you. I feel strong, calm, able to move without shapes and enter your sexual community whose flames I've fed with theory.

Locked in my suburban ranch home.

Wondering if I could ever be a part.

Your ideas about sex are more lucid than any I've heard or read.

There is so much to be learned from listening to you, practicing with you.

I can't ignore my inhibitions and fears but I believe you can.

I wonder if you have been with a man before.

I wonder if you haven't.

I wonder who he was.

I touch your neck with my finger.

You move your leg over mine.

You are staring at me.

I move over you.

You let me.

I kiss you.

You kiss me coquettishly. I kiss you passionately.

You kiss me vigorously.

It is as though you want to be attracted to me.

I kiss you again.

I feel your body move.

I touch your breasts.

You do not object.

I touch your waist.

I lift your shirt and kiss your stomach.

You do not push me away.

I am having an orgasm.

What should I do now?

I like him. He is silly. I touch his thigh with my toe.

He is silent so I am silent. I make faces at him.

He moves over me.

I am experiencing that fear he described.

He tries to kiss me. I kiss his cheek sarcastically.

He kisses me badly. I kiss him hatefully.

I stop kissing him.

I am having trouble breathing.

I remember men.

I lie still.

I am silent with disbelief.

He is not listening to me.

I am afraid of things it would take me all night to explain.

He is breathing quickly.

He can't possibly find this pleasurable.

Stop.

Amy, we walk a minefield as branded lesbians in the patriarchal state.

Amy, our need for each other exposes us to the cruel weathering of language.

I know you are with Becka tonight and the trouble you went to to assure me that you wouldn't have sex with her hurts to remember.

The alcohol has made me wander a maze I normally only see from the overpass and I am trying to make decisions as quickly as his body is.

I want you to come home now, but I want to tell you before you find out.

I am afraid of you, Amy, I am afraid of us dissolving together.

Every friend tries to pour me out and pour themself in.

I want to protect you, Amy, from me, from becoming polluted with my tobacco, damaged by my confidence. I want you to write.

I don't want Amy to be happy. I want Amy to write.

C6. Todorov: Narrator > Character

Narrator > Character is Todorov's term for the omniscient narrator "(where the narrator knows more than the character, or more exactly says more than any of the characters knows)" or, more exactly says more than she says any of the characters knows. Pouillon calls this "vision from behind." Genette calls this "nonfocalized narrative" or "narrative with zero focalization." (*Story and Discourse* 189) Todorov also proposes Narrator = Character (where the narrator knows as much as the character), and Narrator < Character (where the narrator knows less than the character). Mathematically, this would appear to account for every possibility. It does not, however, distinguish *how much* or *what* more the character or narrator knows. The knowledge a narrator might have that a character doesn't could include the character's repressed memories, how the story ends, or even that the character is fictional. Todorov's model can also be complicated by including the narratee, implied author, implied reader, author and reader as being more or less knowledgeable than the others.[33]

C6 has four columns: all variations on point of view of a narrator "fixed" on Professor Chrzastowski as he walks with Dominique to her apartment. Column 1 is Narrator = Character external: it is what an invisible observer, camera, or fly would witness. In column 2, Narrator > Character external: specifically, the narrator knows more about the setting. The narrator knows what is inside the houses they pass. Column 3 is Narrator = Character internal: it is Professor Chrzastowski's narrated monologue. That it is a narrated monologue rather than a summary of his thoughts is indicated by the word "this" in reference to the P.J. Harvey song (otherwise the narrator is referring to a song that has not been mentioned and is not present) and by the stylistic shift to the exasperated run-on sentence. Column 4 is Narrator > Character internal: the narrator is summarizing thoughts that Professor Chrzastowski is not consciously aware of.

---

33   Both Monterroso's "Leopoldo: His Labors" and Borges' "Pierre Menard: Author of Don Quixote" would seem to be Author > Narrator < Reader. The author and (hopefully) reader are aware that the story is actually very silly. This is the essence of deadpan comedy.

C8.

I know you won't accept my apology.

I once wrote that said that sex is a symbolic, not a physical act.

I know that these speculations don't interest you.

I read that poem she sent you.

I'm glad you pointed out that it alternates vowels and consonants, I never would have noticed.

It certainly shows traces of Ebert.

Theresa, yeah, how did you..?

I'm glad you didn't lock me out of the house or anything.

I guess I wish you were mad. Or something.

You accept your marriage with me as an exile. You don't tell me about your teaching anymore. I've gone from thinking that I'm not smart enough to thinking that you think I'm not smart enough to thinking that you need to establish me as not smart enough to contradict plenty of evidence to the contrary to thinking that you're hiding something to knowing that you're hiding something to thinking that you aren't even aware that you're hiding something. I'm not sure you're aware that I am. The way you sigh over herbal tea when you get home is your way of telling me that you can't talk to me. The way you slow yourself with sleeping pills before you fall into bed is your way of telling me you aren't attracted to me. This is your way of telling me you know I'm having an affair with my yoga instructor. Isn't it?

Amy... Unlock the door.

Amy he and I have nothing to do with you and I. He and I had a wonderful conversation. We talked about ways of metaphorically constructing a sexual act as an independent, intelligent, mutual decision. We held hands. Then we had a sexual encounter which failed to be independent mutual and intelligent. But that would take practice. He seemed really nervous and inexperienced. I panicked. It wasn't pleasant. I need to think about it. He's kind of a dork. Why am I saying these things? I don't know what to tell you. I met him in the first place to talk about you. Amy? I never would have thought you'd do this. I don't see how it could be the sex. I was there, I know: it wasn't that important. It can't be the sex. It can't be. It must be the narrative.

C7. Mazza: Allen

In C5 Professor Chrzastowski and Dominique's conversation in the bar is narrated in four columns. The two columns on the left are Professor Chrzastowski and the two columns on the left are Dominique. All four columns are Narrator = Character. The inner columns are unattributed dialogue and the outer columns are sparse interior monologue. This is reminiscent of a scene in Woody Allen's film *Annie Hall* in which a dialogue between two characters is accompanied by subtitles indicating their thoughts, which diverge from their conversation in various unexpected and predictable ways.[34] C7 is an extension of that idea, with the characters' actions replacing their dialogue. Some of the actions are indeed thoughts, but the outermost columns reflect on the events of the scene much more distantly. They are further developments of the characters' contradictory metaphor systems.

This is the scene I expected when I began reading Mazza's "Is It Sexual Harassment Yet?"

To highlight their miscommunications, I wrote Dominique's description of Professor Chrzastowski in the third person and his description of her in the second person.

---

34   RS—This is reminiscent also of Kundera in *The Unbearable Lightness of Being*.

C8. Reagan et al.: Person

I have always considered first, second, and third person interchangeable. In writing or rewriting a scene my choice does not significantly limit what it is possible to narrate. I find this true of the plural as well.[35] The trick is in making sure that the second and third person remain fixed on a single character. In the third (person) column of C8, Dominique slides into the first and third person frequently.

> Identifying pronouns by person helps the writer avoid illogical shifts from one person to another. A common error is to shift from the third person to the second person. (Reagan et al. 302)[36]

One of the fundamental metaphors of narratology is the narrative as sentence. What this metaphor reveals is that a narrative is a linguistic structure and can often be summarized in a sentence.[37] What this metaphor conceals is that a narrative is composed of sentences and that a narrative is identified by semantic features rather than syntactic ones.[38] The illusion it creates is that a narrative tries to communicate its message following strict conventions so that it is easily understood. This metaphor maps syntax onto semantics. Todorov, according to Scholes, maps nouns onto characters, adjectives onto traits and verbs onto their actions (89). Genette adapts Todorov's ideas and uses the properties of the verb to classify "the problems of the narrative in three categories:" "tense," "mood," and "voice." (29) In 1966, Barthes shows that the sentence (as understood by linguists) as a metaphor for narrative reveals that narrative has a hierarchy of "levels." From Benviste

35   Georges Perec's *Things: A Story of the Sixties* is written in the third person plural. This has at least two interesting effects. First: it narrates the life of a man and a woman but by keeping in the plural Perec is never forced to rely on a single gendered pronoun. The male and female character are often indistinguishable and the story becomes inadvertently feminist. Second: the pronoun "they" seems to lose its focus on the two characters at time and their actions seem to become that of a mob or an entire generation. The story is a grammar exercise. The final chapter is in the future tense: "But it will not be easy for them to escape from their own story." (Perec 120)

36   Here's no finesse, no silk tie, no Ramirez floating on his knee, no linen program, no one to appreciate what he brings, nothing fine at all, just this messy business of life where all things come too late and find you no longer ready, standing in the center of your own dream in a fool nightshirt with an electrified two-by-four in your fist and six skinny steel strings on which nothing lovely could ever be played, here, at this test of the vitality of a man's delusions: will you do it now when there is no longer anything to be gained? Will you do it now just because, such as things are, this is going to be your only chance? Will you do it to say death wasn't the only reason? Will you do it for children?

        Of course you will. (Berry 80)

37   RS—These two propositions do not necessarily follow from one another and while certain narratologists are fond of the latter, the more fundamental and significant claim is the former.

38   RS—According to Barthes, a narrative is identified by both. The *distributional* corresponds to syntax and the *integrational* to semantics.

D1.

A crumpled cigarette butt and a tearstain outside the door.

A copy of her finished thesis on the edge of the table.

Her desecrated ashtray beside her computer, the keyboard blackened from use.

A deep trunk of writing beneath the table.

The *Princeton Guide to Poetry and Poetics*, the *OED* (opened to "hermeneutic"), and a medical atlas.

A list of words that alternate consonants and vowels.

An open window.

A broken bottle in an alleyway.

OVERTHROW PATRIARCHY scrawled in silver lipstick on a bank.

A silk scarf snagged on a barbed wire fence.

An empty film canister sitting on a rafter of an abandoned barn.

Footprints through a dirt field beneath constellations named after women.

A marbled pink comb by the railroad tracks.

A handwritten poem taped to the side of a boxcar

> (but
> And she tried to tell me her dream that I would be satisfied with her/that
> the importance I ascribed to having an actively nonmonogamous sexual
> life would fade/that in her mind I would find a community as diverse as
> any/in her hands would be revealed a language of new gestures/in her
> face were unfamiliar expressions waiting to emerge/in her voice were
> the murmurs of many/that she had been building/she had been learning/
> had been storing/was ready/but).

A jeweled stickpin covered with marijuana resin in the trash in the lavatory of a Greyhound bus.

he adapts the terms distributional and integrational ("Introduction" 86). Distributional elements (horizontal) must occur in a particular sequence (HER, ACT). Integrational elements need not (REF, SEM, SYM).

D2.

To: "Amy Johnson" <ajjohns@austen.edu >
From: "Dominique X. Roussel" <dxrouss@austen.edu> Fri Apr 26 10:51:09 1996
X-Mailer: ELM [version 2.4 PL23] Mime-Version: 1.0 Content-Type: text/plain; charset=US-ASCII
Re: Re: Re: Re: Re: Re: Re: I love you (FWD)

>>>>>I never thought you'd leave, which I guess doesn't explain why I locked you out of the
>>>>>apartment. Sorry.

>>>>What makes you think you decided to do that? What else could you have done?

>>>>>>Do you mind if I don't tell you the true story? Your reaction has made it even more distorted
>>>>>>than it was when it happened. Any explanation I give you will be an explanation to you, not an
>>>>>>analysis. Even I

>>>It's a relief actually. It's an insane world and it wants to kill us. We aren't prepared for it. All we do
>>>is kiss and write. We're too afraid of losing each other to apply seriously to any doctoral programs.
>>>Neither of us has a job and you have no work experience. The longer you stay in the bathtub, the >>>colder
the air is when you get out. I felt trapped.

>>Strange, I felt exposed. To you certainly, but also to the world. I'm used to being considered a dyke,
>>but to have a lover is to let the world see you care. Uncomfortable and vulnerable.

>>>>>>can't remember it correctly anymore. I'm not sure what I told Debra but I'm sure he will
>>>>>>correct it. In fact, I can't remember anything from eleventh grade through my Bachelors but I'm
>>>>>>starting to remember what I've tried to forget. Let me know if you still want to be friends or
>>>>>>lovers. Otherwise I will vanish like a hit of marijuana in a hurricane.

>>>>>Cut it out. Your shrapnel is embedded in me for good. And I doubt you'll ever smoke over your

>>>>That's not what I'm talking about at all. In fact, my addictions are crumbling beneath me.
>>>>Memories are rumbling to the surface. Did you know I had an uncle?

>>>>>memory of me, no matter how hard you try. Your memory is fine. You're inventing a limp to fit
>>>>>the crutch. Where the hell are you?

>>>>I'm in Lake Forest. Mom is in Paris at a meeting of the Oulipo. I told the administrators that I'm
>>>>living on the streets of Chicago and using the computer in the public library. Lies. Given the only
>>>>two social narratives to choose from, one where I am a victim, two where I am a seductress, I want
>>>>to establish the former. I did hop a boxcar, but only as far as the bus station. I'm not coming back.
>>>>I'm going to fax my thesis in. I'm sure I can convince them to let me have my defense over the
>>>>internet. If you want, come and get me after you graduate.

>>>What are you writing?

>>I have been leaving anonymous poetry on police cars, in newspaper machines, taped to the aisles at
>>supermarkets, in business reply envelopes, in books deep in the library. I am trying to separate my
>>desire to write from my desire to show off. My anonymity is ultimately not any more responsible than
>>my narcissism, but seductive. I could never write with you watching for some reason.

>Shouldn't you be trying to get published?

That will be my next exercise.

D1. Chynoweth: Gender

Why did I give certain of the characters female names and clothing? This second point is especially baffling: I don't think Dominique is the sort of person who would carry a purse (C4) or lipstick (D1).

My esteemed friend and best colleague Danielle Chynoweth recently led a workshop on gender problems in fiction. She provided a list of conventions in patriarchal realist fiction that serve to introduce semiotic (Genette) actant—objects or receivers of more thoroughly developed male character's sexual desires—(Greimas) female characters to index (Barthes 1966) a sexy mood according to established cultural codes (Barthes 1974). To put it coherently, there is a tradition of female characters who are "flat," frequently unnamed, usually undeveloped, described visually, used as a sexy background, only in the story to motivate and constrain the central male characters, beautiful, naïve, helpless, molested, beaten, and raped. A story which portrays violence against women uncritically— which is not *about* violence towards women—will frequently, intentionally or otherwise, poeticize, glamorize, and promote this violence.

This story was written to address some of these problems. This story consists of a solution atop a problem atop a solution. The first, bottom solution was to give the characters female names and clothing. This is almost the extent of my efforts to establish the characters as women. This is not a story about women or lesbians, but a story about people and lovers with female names and clothing. In addition, I have tried to remove certain indicators of patriarchy as they cropped up. I have named the universities and their buildings (and a bar) after female writers (the real buildings my fictional buildings are based on are named after male politicians). The problem I layered atop this solution was to give Professor Chrzastowski a male pronoun. This is a problem because he is a character in a position of authority, so to establish him as male reasserts the patriarchy the first solution was intended to efface.[39] He is even more problematic because he refers to Debbie as "my wife" and characterizes her poorly as a spiritual person. The final, second solution is the second (person) column in C8, where Debbie is finally given a voice and allowed to critique exactly his poor characterization of her. [40]

---

39   RS—Does representing something necessarily endorse it?
40   DFW—"affair with yoga instructor": "too cheap a joke? It undercuts the grand pathos of Debbie's despair above."

Honorificabilitudinitatibus: a Sonata

1. Repose

Men examined everybody but used one logic.

A man is a male but a woman is a female.
So generalize: genitalize taxonomy.
Not a penis, a vagina
(not an ovary) sexes us.
Is a man a woman or a woman a man?
Is one human, one mimetic?
Is a man a fake model of a woman?
Or is a woman a robotic image to refer
(as a sexeme) to man?
Am I paradoxical? I simulate veracity.

But are we separated, alone? We mix. One model of a family—monogamy—to deter
us. A time for a "we": homolexical. A delicate case: so, monogamy to make sure we get
isolated in a line, to get isolated one woman at a time.

2. Develop

I modulate my motives.
I have love, but a hate.

He monopolizes every vocabulary.
Lexicas are his alone to divide her up in.

I make my music: a facile logological analysis.
I can use my power of "I" to do.
But I lose verisimilitude.

He capitalizes on an ability to maximize his ego.
He can eliminate, wed, erase, delete, desire her.
It is a rare power if one has a name: his.

I defecate misogyny.
My name to be put on a cover: anodyzed.
Academic: I lower anybody.

We run over a woman in a waxy canonical elite limo.

D2. Lakoff: E-mail

No matter how the idea of the character is understood, exalted, or dismissed; is it possible to have a narrative without them? The central character of Dominique is almost entirely unnarrated.[41] I tried to establish her as the central character not through her presence (which is mostly unattributed dialogue) but through the other characters' fascination with her. In the final section of the story—the fourth circle which is fixed on her—she does not appear. In D1 her actions are narrated as a series of objects, traces of walking all night through the town and countryside. D2 is an e-mail message which has been sent back and forth between Dominique (at her mother's house in a prosperous Chicago subdivision) and Amy six times. The original message (the one with the most carats on the left margin) has snowballed as each responded to and interrupted each other's sentences. D2 would appear, from the workshop, to be completely indecipherable. One of ISU's most talented programmers didn't seem to get it (BW), another student assumed it was an on-line chat (SF), yet another student assumed that the last line was the voice of the author rather than Dominique (JH), and the instructor found himself unable to determine who had told Debbie about the encounter between Dominique and her husband (DFW). In an original score, I had planned to put this e-mail message first. It is hard to say what the effect of this would be. According to Genette, it would be a simple anachronism. According to Barthes it might constitute a reversal of the Hermeneutic code and the Code of Actions—an impossibility. Within this e-mail exchange, the poetic, overwritten lines ("too heavy"—DFW) are parts of an argument where Amy and Dominique clash metaphor systems. In the chronological (as opposed to the typographic) sequence of the exchange, the metaphors play themselves out as follows:

D:	"I will vanish like a hit of marijuana in a hurricane" (COMMUNITY = DIFFUSION)
A:	"Your shrapnel is embedded in me for good" (COMMUNITY = FRAGMENTATION)
	"…inventing a limp to fit the crutch" (DRUGS = CRUTCH)
D:	"my addictions are crumbling beneath me" (DRUGS = FOUNDATION)
A:	"I felt trapped" (MONOGAMY = PRISON)
D:	"I felt exposed" (MONOGAMY = SHELTERLESS)

---

41   This avoided a serious problem. There is no way I could narrate from Dominique's point of view convincingly. She is clearly smarter than I. (Dominique > William) [RS—Is this the implied or real author..?]

3. Recapitulate.

We war over an imaginative validity.
We men are limited in an inability to be women.

I made her a catatonic animal, a cute sexy baby pet, a magazine.
Before paralytic ego, now a wizened id.
I made her a novel. A page.

Literature we gave to men.

I made women a topic. I gave women a deliberately feminine timidity to defer every
diminutive minimum. I made her every name we hope we men are not: a woman, a
woman I defer a name to.

4. Coda

Put a woman in every man.

I do.

Nobody separate.

No syzygy but a sun.

Every vowel a semihemidemimonotone.

Synonymy.

Works Cited and Bibliography

Acker, Kathy. *Don Quixote*. New York: Grove Press, 1986.

Auster, Paul. *The New York Trilogy*. New York: Penguin Books, 1986.

Barthes, Roland. "Introduction to the Structural Analysis of Narratives." *Image, Music, Text*. Hill and Wang, 1977.

Barthes, Roland. "Objective Literature: Alain Robbe-Grillet." *Two Novels*. By Alain Robbe-Grillet. New York: Grove Press, 1969. 11-26.

Barthes, Roland. *S/Z*. Trans. Richard Miller. New York: Hill and Wang, 1974.

Berry, R. M. *Plane Geometry and Other Affairs of the Heart*. Normal: Illinois State University, 1985.

Bierce, Ambrose. *Civil War Stories*. New York: Dover, 1984.

Borges, Jorge Luis. *Ficciones*. Emecé Editores, trans. New York: Grove, 1962.

Calvino, Italo. *T Zero*. Trans. William Weaver. San Diego: Harvest/HBJ, 1969.

Chambers, Ross. *Room for Maneuver*. Chicago: University of Chicago, 1991.

Chambers, Ross. *Story and Situation*. Minneapolis: University of Minnesota, 1984.

Chatman, Seymour. *Story and Discourse*. Ithaca: Cornell University Press, 1989.

Chatman, Seymour. "Voice." *Narrative/Theory*. Longman, 1996.

Cohn, Dorit. "Narrated Monologue." *Narrative/Theory*. Longman, 1996.

Coward, Rosalind, and John Ellis. *Language and Materialism*. London: Routledge & Kegan Paul, 1977.

De Certeau, Michel. *The Practice of Everyday Life*. Trans. Steven Rendall. Berkeley: University of California Press, 1984.

Foucault, Michel. *The Order of Things*. Trans. unknown. New York: Random House, 1970.

Genette, Gérard. *Narrative Discourse*. Trans. Jane E. Lewin. Ithaca: Cornell University Press, 1980.

Genette, Gérard. «Order, Duration, Frequency.» *Narrative/Theory*. Longman, 1996.

Irigaray, Luce. *This Sex Which is Not One*. Trans. Catherine Porter. Ithaca: Cornell University Press, 1985.

Johnson, Mark. *The Body in the Mind*. Chicago: The University of Chicago Press, 1987.

Lakoff, George. "Metaphor and War: The Metaphor System Used to Justify War in the Persian Gulf."

Lakoff, George, and Mark Turner. *More Than Cool Reason*. Chicago: University of Chicago, 1989.

Martin, Wallace. *Recent Theories of Narrative*. Ithaca: Cornell University Press, 1987

Marx, Karl. *The Marx-Engels Reader*. New York: W.W. Norton, 1978.

Mazza, Chris. Is It Sexual *Harassment* Yet? Normal: FC2, 1998.

Mitchell, W.J.T. *On Narrative*. Chicago: University of Chicago Press, 1981.

Monterroso, Augusto. *Complete Works and Other Stories*. Trans. Edith Grossman. Austin: University of Texas, 1995.

Perec, Georges. *Things: A Story of the Sixties*. Trans. David Bellos. Boston: Godine, 1990.

Pynchon, Thomas. *The Crying of Lot 49*. New York: Harper and Row, 1986.

Reagan, Sally Barr et al. *Writing From A to Z*. Mountain View, California: Mayfield, 1994.

Rimmon-Kenan, Shlomith. *Narrative Fiction*. London: Methuen, 1983.

Saunders, Rebecca. "Time Above and Below the Liminal: Tempo and Pace as Functions of Literary Rhythm."

Scholes, Robert. *Semiotics and Interpretation*. New Haven: Yale University Press, 1982.

Sturman, Marianne. *Cliffs Notes on Don Quixote*. Lincoln, Nebraska: Cliffs Notes Inc., 1964.

Swenson, May. *In Other Words*. New York: Alfred A. Knopf, 1982.

Ulmer, Gregory L. "'A Night at the Text': Roland Barthes's Marx Brothers." *Yale French Studies* 73 (1987): 38-57.

Wallace, David Foster. *The Broom of the System*. New York: Penguin, 1987.

Watt, Ian. *The Rise of the Novel*. University of California, 1957.

Dave,

Class last week brought up a number of interesting questions. Questions like: what the hell am I doing with my life? I seem to have written myself back into a corner of my own brain so remote that not even you and Jason and a team of English graduate students working together with searchlights, helicopters, and bloodhounds, can find me. My writing has improved so much since I entered graduate school that there is no longer anyone qualified to read it. In class for the first time I received more sadness than hostility: a room full of blank faces, letters which read like page-long apologies, and meanwhile Jason accusing me of misrepresenting theories I wasn't, in many cases, even trying to represent. I've seldom gone to so much trouble to do such a small segment of a possible readership so little good. This is quite a way to end nearly a decade of intermittent college writing workshops, and quite a way to say goodbye to the only readers I will ever be guaranteed.

Well, that was how this letter began. After working on the paper it occurred to me that I actually *know* what the hell I'm doing. I know *exactly* what I'm doing. I'm going broke and insane trying to teach the English language to dance. It's a good life. And you needn't worry that I am going to turn around and try to write like Carver or Updike. The sort of bad ideas you've seen me try – a story with one form of punctuation per page, a story where the number of words per sentence decreases by two every paragraph, a story where every two adjacent words have at least one letter in common – have taken years to contrive. (But I didn't do anything like that in *this* story and I feel kind of bad to see that you started counting the number of words in each sentence, apparently out of sheer desperation.) Though there is not yet a place for these ideas in literature (nothing ending with -ism) they are easy to understand and explain (the ideas, not the writing) and part of a world of writing practices useful in that they can force inspiration in blocked writers and constrain the impassioned diuretic flow of clichés in confident writers. In a workshop I am both. I started writing like this, in fact, because of a workshop. I needed decision-making criteria so that, when I received a flood of individually contradictory but collectively discouraging instructions about what to change, I would have the original structure as a guide to know which advice I could use and which I couldn't. I don't like the fact that I now write stories with Roland Barthes jokes which perhaps one percent of English speaking people know aren't funny. This is not my new direction. What I want to do for my thesis is carry the unnamable formal ideas I referred to above to their unnatural conclusions. I want use biology, economics, the contemporary theory of metaphor, and Dr. Seuss. At the same time, unless my writing is (if not emotionally rich) readable and relevant to people, I am not doing what I want yet. Intellectual masturbation is an interesting metaphor. Only according to a conventional metaphor system which posits mind and body as opposites can it even *be* a metaphor. Masturbation is literally an intellectual experience. I am into formal stuntpilotry for its own sake: not because I want to be remembered for breaking the text barrier, but because I like being high, fast, and upside down. Structures precede stories. I know when the structures work but I don't know when the stories "work." When you suggest that the formal structure must be relevant to the story, well, I agree, but what the hell are we each talking about? That's a huge conversation and an interesting one. Let's have it. Until then I'll be in my room reading *Life: a User's Manual* and trying to move as little as possible to conserve calories.
    William

P. S. Please stop calling me "Bill."

I am grateful to all the participants of the fiction writing workshop English 447.02 (Spring 1996) at Illinois State University who gave me feedback on the story. I have chosen to cite them without their permission. I am also grateful to Dr. Rebecca Saunders (English 404: Narratology) whose stimulating curriculum and mild encouragement enabled me to write an unconventional essay. I have quoted their written comments (including an entire letter to me, included as a postface) and paraphrased their spoken comments. I refer to them by their initials throughout:

BB	Becky Bradway	RB	Ronn Byrd
KD	Kim Dozier	SF	Steve Fast
WG	William Gillespie	JH	Jason Hammel
FM	Frank Marquart	BS	Ben Slotky
RT	Rosemarie Thornton	BW	Bill Weakley

RS	Rebecca Saunders
DFW	David Wallace

Thanks to all who have tried to teach this.
A very special thanks to Jakob Kappel Peterson, Denmark, for a close reading.

The Story That Teaches You How To Write It. Second Spineless Edition. 2009.
$10. ISBN 0-9724244-0-7. ISBN-13 978-0-9724244-0-0.
Library of Congress Control Number: 2009907972

SPINELESS BOOKS  PROVIDENCE